Cherry Twist

A CHERRY PI MYSTERY, VOLUME 2

Jennifer Stone

This edition published in 2020 by Farrago,
an imprint of Duckworth Books Ltd
13 Carrington Road, Richmond, TW10 5AA, United Kingdom

www.farragobooks.com

ISBN: 978-1-78842-167-6

Printed in Great Britain by Clays Ltd.

For Melissa – happy now?

Prologue

Nadiya Slipchenko swirls her long, multi-layered flamenco gown in both hands. She throws a haughty look over her shoulder and walks away. Suddenly, Alexi Bondareyev runs after her and spins her round to face him. As the music increases in tempo, they both move more quickly. He flings her against the target board which has been brought on by two of the others. She writhes against it, appearing to beg for help. Alexi reaches behind him and pulls out three knives which he shows to the crowd who have gathered. He throws one of the knives at the board. It is meant to whistle past Nadiya's head but instead she screams and clamps her hand to her ear. Already, dark red blood is seeping through her cupped fingers.

'Stop!' Chris Gordon, the producer, runs on along with several other people. The music continues. 'I said stop! Nic, stop the fucking music, mate.'

Eventually, the music dies away. Between her sobs, Nadiya hisses at Chris, 'Can you not see? Someone has it in for me! This is no accident; they are trying to kill me.'

Alexi rushes over and says, 'I do not understand how this has happened. This knife, it is supposed to be a false knife, it is a prop. It should not have cut you.'

One of the floor assistants runs over to the board where the slightly bloody knife is embedded in the target. He pulls it out and holds it aloft like a budget Excalibur. 'It's a real knife.'

Chris can't believe his eyes; he walks over to the assistant and takes the knife from his hand. He feels the weight and the sharpness of the blade. The assistant is right. It is a real knife.

Nadiya is led away but as she goes she turns and says to Chris, 'This is the second time, Chris. I want someone to investigate. I want her from *The Caravan*, with the cakes. How is she called? Cherry Hinton. You bring me Cherry Hinton or I will no longer dance for you on your programme.'

Chapter One

Kelsey and I were sitting in the green room of the set for Expose's flagship programme *The Dance is Right*. We were well excited because we'd both spent many hours watching the programme and commenting on the performers from the comfort of various sofas. Chris Gordon, the producer, had invited me there as his guest because he had a proposition for me.

I told him that so long as it wasn't yet another feeble attempt to get me to appear on *Watch My Ex Having Sex* along with my sort of ex, Jacob Stow, then I would consider coming along. Naturally, the minute I'd casually mentioned it to Kelsey, she'd bitten my arm off, so, here we were.

The green room overlooked the famous dance floor where professional dancers and celebrities (who were mainly a cast of people who'd appeared on other Expose shows) competed to guess the cost of various household items and dance in strangely themed routines such as 'luggage week'. Chris Gordon had purchased the rights to *The Price is Right* and was looking for a way to revive the format and create a Saturday night 'family-focused' show to rival some of the major channels. Bizarrely, watching barely recognisable celebrities guessing the cost of a Zanussi washing machine with enhanced spin features before performing a jive inspired by said appliance was a huge hit.

Since it was a Thursday afternoon, there wasn't really anyone around. The band were rehearsing at the side of the floor and a few men and women dressed in black with hipster hair and walkie talkies were flitting around putting down tape and chatting to one another.

''Ere, where are all dancers?' demanded Kelsey through her mango smoothie. 'I didn't come all this way to see a band play the same eight bars ten times over. Where's Belinda Price and Jason Devine?'

I was about to point out that I'd made no promises regarding the quality of the stars we might encounter during our visit when Kelsey grabbed my arm and hissed, 'Look, look over there. It's Nadiya Slipchenko – it's actually her. Oh my God, she's amazing.'

Into the bar walked a woman of almost perfect proportions. She was tall and slim; beneath her skin-tight black leotard and practice skirt, every muscle in her body seemed to ripple with supple expectation. Despite the fact her hair was scraped back into a severe bun and her face was make-up free, she had the kind of beauty that made you lean back and simultaneously regret leaving the house without a spare bag to put your head in. I really hoped that she was there just to get a drink and we could simply admire her from afar, but it seemed that she was making her way over.

'Hello,' she cried, almost in amazement, 'I thought that Chris was pulling my arm when he said that he would get you here. I thought to myself, *That man is a liar*, but he has. You are here.'

'Yes,' I said awkwardly. 'I'm here.' I was none the wiser as to why someone like Nadiya would want my company. It seemed unlikely that Chris Gordon would have done anything that didn't involve personal gain on his part. I really hoped that she wasn't shagging him in some misguided belief that it would benefit her.

'I am Nadiya Slipchenko. You are Miss Cherry Hinton, yes?'

'Yes, pleased to meet you, Nadiya.' I held out my hand awkwardly and she grasped it.

'No, Miss Cherry Hinton, it is I who am pleased to meet you. I feel less scared already. This will help my dancing.'

Kelsey had been rendered mute by this exchange. I saw her just staring at Nadiya's perfect skin, dazzled by its smoothness. I also could not think of anything helpful to say. I wasn't sure what Chris had told her but I was unclear on how my presence would improve the world champion Latin and ballroom dancer's ability to create a dance based on household linens and towels. She pressed on, 'And you are now my friend so you must call me Nads.'

'Righty ho! And you don't need to, er, call me… call me Cherry. Cherry is fine.' I was so smooth.

'Ah, Cherry, Nads. There you are. You've met already I see.' Chris Gordon's oily voice rang out across the room and for the first time in my life, I was pleased to see him. He marched over and slid his hand down Nads's back.

I saw a flicker of disgust move across her face before she broke into a smile. 'Now, Chris, the others, they say you are a liar and that you will not pay for Miss Cherry Hinton but I say, no. Chris is a good man who want the best for his dancers. And I am right. I thank you for this.' Then she leant forward and lightly kissed him just above his dry-looking beard. She had quite possibly practised avoiding the greasiest patches of skin around his nose as she seemed to home in on the one normal-looking bit of his face. 'I must go and stretch. We will talk soon.'

I think that we all watched her walk away but I recovered most quickly. 'So, Chris, what was that all about? How am I supposed to help the best dancer in the world? I'm sure you've not asked me here to share the secrets of my rumba.'

Kelsey snorted more loudly than was necessary and Chris grinned. 'Ah well, no, it's not your dancing I'm interested in right now, but you know, always looking for celebs to appear on the show.'

'Chris, get to the point.' I'd had quite enough of Chris's antics when I met him earlier in the year and clashed with him over my investigation of a murder in the Big Blubber House. He was a dodgy producer then and from the looks of it, nothing much had changed.

Nadiya was down on the main dance floor now. She bent over gracefully and began stretching. I wished that I looked that good with my bum in the air. We all stood on the balcony, mesmerised by Nadiya as she twisted, lunged and extended. She called something to the band leader and 'Between the Sheets' by The Isley Brothers started up. Of course, I reminded myself, it was household linens week. She began pacing out what was presumably her dance and I reluctantly turned back to Chris.

Chris scrubbed at his head and I fought the urge to slap his hands away.

'Yes, yes, of course. Right, well, you know what these, er, creative types are like. Especially the, er, er, what's the PC term nowadays?'

'Foreign ones!' interjected Kelsey.

'Yes, they are a bit more… temperamental and artistic. And, the thing is, Nadiya has got it into her head that—'

Suddenly, there was an almighty crash from the dance floor below followed by terrified high-pitched screaming. We all craned over the balcony. Where Nadiya had been standing, there was now a crater in the dance floor. In it was a heavy hook which had fallen from the roof space and was embedded in the ground. It was so heavy that it had smashed through the wood and even though we were a distance away, the concrete was visible beneath it. A cluster of the black-clad people were now gathered around Nadiya, who, unsurprisingly, was the one screaming.

Chris Gordon made it down the steps much faster than I expected. He threw his arms around Nadiya and crooned murmurs of comfort. Kelsey and I walked over quickly and inspected the floor. Even the concrete beneath looked cracked and damaged.

One of the hipster types approached and slipped his headphones over the back of his head. He looked at the floor in horror and said, 'Fucking hell, that's gunna take some fixing. Steve's gunna throw a fucking fit when he sees this. Fuck me. What a fucking mess.'

I waited for Chris to say something but Kelsey was in there quicker.

'Oy, she nearly fuckin' died. You not bothered about that?'

His manbun shook indignantly. 'Yes, of course I am—'

'Well then, shut up about the floor and sort out some sort of medical help before she suffocates in his armpit.'

She was right – Chris had her so firmly wedged against him, her ability to breathe was a serious concern.

Hipster Type whipped out his radio and, in his mockney accent, summoned some back-up in the form of two women who appeared in seconds with much more appropriate responses.

'Oh my God, Nads, babe, are you OK?'

'We'll totes get you some cannabis oil, hun.'

They prised her away from Chris's reluctant grasp and she was ushered off. She looked over her shoulder at Chris and shouted through her tears, 'You believe me now? Someone is trying to kill me!'

Chapter Two

'It says here that she last won the Latin World Championship in 2016 at the Royal Albert Hall and that apparently an old injury from when she was a child has prevented her from competing on the world stage again.'

'Hmmm.' I wasn't paying complete attention to Kelsey's Google research. Since I'd set up my business as a private investigator and supplemented that with selling cakes on Brentwood High Street, Kelsey had appointed herself my glamorous assistant. This was despite the fact she was often the source of my problems rather than a solution. I turned the cake-based replica of Brentwood Cathedral, resplendent with controversial gold railings, on its stand. I was sure that the retiring cardinal would love it.

'How do you even think she got that body? Do you think she eats keto?'

'What's a keto?'

'Not "a" keto; it's not a thing, it's a lifestyle where your body basically eats its own fat. Like, *everyone* is eating keto.'

I got my fine brush out to touch up the windows of the cathedral. 'I thought everyone was clean vegan…'

Kelsey sighed dramatically. 'That was last year. Now everyone is eating keto. Jesus, Cherry, you're so, like, out of touch with dietary trends.'

'Yeah well, since every dietary trend seems to avoid cake consumption, it's a wonder that I don't go out of business and yet, here we are. Funny that, don't you think?'

'Anyway' – she dragged a pink sparkly nail down the screen of her phone – 'what you need to be focusing on is if you are going to take up Chris's offer or not. I mean, you'd be a fool not to but then this is the same woman who has turned down hot Jacob Stow sixty billion times so…'

I carefully squared off the last window with the tip of my brush and put it in the sink to wash up. Despite running two businesses out of it, my shop was pretty much unchanged. A massive cheque from a very grateful client had paid for top-of-the-range coolers and a KitchenAid in cherry red that I'd been coveting for a long time but other than that, it was still nestled neatly between Pandora and the O2 shop and had barely any room inside. I liked it that way.

The case of Nadiya Slipchenko was an interesting one. Made especially interesting by being there when it all kicked off.

'I won't tell a lie, Kels, it's got a lot more going for it than looking for stolen chihuahuas and stalking dodgy nannies round Thorndon Country Park. I'm just worried.'

'Tell me you're not about to say, "I'm just worried about upsetting PC Jacob Stow if he is already involved".'

Was I that transparent?

'No,' I said, thinking quickly of a good lie, 'I was going to say that I was worried about not keeping up with my cakes and also, Jacob is a DS, not a PC.'

She totally ignored my remark about Jacob. 'I thought that was why you employed D'arcy Onions.'

'Why do you have to keep saying her name like that?'

'Like what; that is her name, isn't it? D'arcy Onions.'

'Yeah but it's like you're taking the mick or something.' Or she was jealous that I had an actual employee that I paid and got on with?

'It's a pretty stupid name, though. Like a character from a kids' programme or something.'

'Yeah, well, she can't help that.'

Kelsey scanned around the shop and pointed at a plate of cakes in the window. 'What are they? They're new.' Before I could answer, she was off her seat and ramming one into her mouth. 'Mmm, that's good, sort of sandy in a good way.'

'It's a Frinton Fancy, like a French Fancy, but I've used sugar to create a sandy layer between the cream and the fondant. Anyway, back to the conversation, I'm worried about doing an investigation so close to Christmas. It's a prime time to be selling cakes. I've got this Southminceter Pie Cake that I've been trialling and I've just perfected my Ferrero Rochfords.'

Kelsey looked at me. I could feel myself gabbling for excuses. She raised a feathered eyebrow. 'So nothing whatsoever to do with Jacob, then? You two are all good, yeah?'

'Yes. We're just taking it easy, seeing how it goes. No pressure. Dead casual.'

She smirked at me and wiped her mouth on the back of her hand. 'Yeah right!'

Chapter Three

The last time I'd been in this office, I'd struck a deal that resulted in Chris Gordon and the channel for which he produced shows, Expose, being exposed (an irony which never failed to amuse me) as nasty people who preyed on the unhappiness of the citizens of Essex. Little had changed apart from, this time, Chris wanted something from me. Chris was nothing more than a greasy, sleazy businessman who had tapped into the somewhat questionable talents of the people who lived in Brentwood and surrounding areas in order to make depressingly cheap and tacky programmes. He had a plethora of shows running at the same time, but *The Dance is Right* was the biggest.

'OK, Chris. I won't tell a lie, I'm slightly interested. Tell me one thing, though – you didn't orchestrate that hook falling down as part of some sick ploy to get me involved?'

'Cherry, darling, am I the kind of man who would do that? Seriously, love, I am shocked that you think I'd stoop so low.' He shook his head sadly and steepled his fingers against his beard in what I assumed was an act of sincerity.

'Chris, there's nothing you could do that would surprise me when it comes to getting a good story or better viewing figures. I know you too well, mate.'

He laughed good-naturedly and spun his phone around on the table. 'So, here it is. About three weeks ago when the season had its teaser opening, there they all are, rehearsing for the opening number. Nadiya and her partner Alexi are doing this, like, circus-themed section…'

'Is he her boyfriend or just a dance partner?'

'Well, now, it's interesting you should say that. Your old friend Julia Scofield reports in the *Essex Chronicle* that Nadiya split up with him because he was knobbing Belinda Price.'

I winced at his expression and he noticed. 'Come on, Cherry, we're all grown-ups here. Get over yourself. Anyways, the choreographer, Damien Spiritwind—'

'No way is that his real name. You are kidding me, right?' I seriously could not believe that anyone would call themselves that. He sounded like a pretentious fool. I mentally put money on him having a long, well-cared for beard (with its own special kit), chunky beads and a linen boiler suit.

'Do you actually want to know what's happened or are we gonna bitch about people's names all morning? I know I'm asking you for a favour but there are other people I could go to.' He picked up his phone and actually started scrolling.

'OK, OK, keep your hair on. I'm listening, no more interruptions.'

'So Damien Spiritwind, the top West End choreographer and founding father of the Spiritwind Foundation for Disabled Kiddies or whatnot, had created this section where Alexi is supposed to chuck some knives at Nadiya while she writhes about on the target board looking all sexy and vulnerable and that. The knives are supposed to represent the danger of love or something. So, there they are rehearsing this bit and all of a sudden, she starts screaming and her ear's like gushing blood everywhere. Someone picks up this knife he's whanged at her and it's only fucking real. It's a fucking real knife. So I'm like, where's the polystyrene one? And it's only gone and disappeared.'

It sounded pretty unbelievable to me that Alexi wouldn't have noticed the difference between a prop knife and a real knife. 'Who gave him the knife, how did that bit work?'

'Well now, here's the thing. He had built into his costume, which was a trad paso outfit with the cape and that, this sort of pockety bit where the knife was kept. So, all he had to do in the dance was reach behind him, pull it out and chuck it at her. Which he did.'

Now for the killer question that would determine my involvement in a case which, I had to admit, sounded really exciting compared to what I'd been up to lately. 'And did you call the police?'

Chris threw back his head and laughed. I could see all his fillings, black against his mossy yellow teeth. 'Cherry, darling, just say it. What's with all this pussyfooting around, eh? Come on, say it…'

I sighed; did everyone have the power to read my mind? Even gross Chris Gordon? 'Is Jacob Stow already involved?'

'There, that wasn't so hard was it? The short answer is no. Loverboy couldn't care less. I called him straight away. He comes down, takes a look around. Takes a particularly long hard look at Nadiya and Belinda if you know what I mean… hahahaha.'

'Thanks for that, Chris, I get the idea.' Wanker. I fought down the stabby pain in my tummy at the thought of Jacob ogling the perfect Nadiya and the stunning Belinda, who hosted the show.

'And then he decides it's an accident with the props department. No one's got a reason to kill her so, business as usual.'

'OK, so we've got the knife three weeks ago and then the hook last Thursday. Is that it in terms of so-called attempts on Nadiya's life?' I flipped over the pages of my notebook to check the details I had already pulled together. I wanted to be certain of all of the facts before I committed to any of Chris's dodgy deals.

He flicked open a clipboard that was sitting on his messy desk and riffled through the pages for a moment. 'Er, no, there's one more incident. I wasn't there so I'm just checking this note from Nic Johnston; she's the band leader and she saw the whole thing. It happened during the warm-up for the second live show. It's what made me call you on the Monday. Here you go.'

He presented me with a scribbled side of A4 which read:

I was just warming the band up with a few bars of 'The Great Escape' when Nads and Felix came down on the floor. She tells me that they need to go over a section of their dance again and so we start playing their song, 'You Spin Me Right Round' – it's an American Smooth so it works OK if we play it with a slightly slower tempo, I told the drummer to aim for a bossa nova beat and the trumpets to swing the quavers a bit. So we're playing the refrain and no one is filming them or anything cos we're just warming up and doing last-minute bits. Then, out of nowhere, while he's spinning her round this massive camera that we use for tracking shots when you want to get the whole cast in, comes flying towards them. I try to call out but the music's too loud and it happened so quick that there's nothing I can do. He sees it, though, at the last minute and dives them both sideways. It sort of clipped her foot and she starts screaming. It definitely looked like someone pushed it. There's no way it could have come for them that fast by accident.

I read it all a couple of times. Three near misses – one I'd witnessed last week with my own eyes. No wonder poor Nadiya was convinced someone was trying to kill her. I'd be pretty worried myself. 'Er, Felix? As in Nadiya's celebrity partner in the competition, Felix?'

Chris Gordon looked at me, surprised. 'Felix? Felix Stow? He's Jacob's brother. How did you not know that?'

I certainly knew who Felix Stow was and the mention of his name made me feel a little bit sick.

It's lunchtime at school but I'm not hungry. I've arranged to meet him in the DT room. I can't actually believe that he agreed to meet me. I didn't even know that he knew me but Jo and Michelle cornered him at break by the lockers and asked if he wanted to meet me for a lunch date and he said yes. A sixth former said yes. To me.

I've been given a makeover in the loos by Michelle, who has the whole Rimmel collection and some well nice Clinique stuff that she's nicked off her mum. I've got tonnes of mascara on and I smell like a dewberry!

I see him through the door pretending to be working on his picnic bench project. I'm holding my DT folder just in case I get asked by Mr Handley what I'm doing there. I push open the door and walk in.

'Hi.' He smiles just like Jacob does and I feel all hot and floaty.

'Hello.' I try to think of something interesting to say. 'I like your bench. It's a nice colour. A nice woody colour.'

'That'll be the wood then.' He doesn't say it sarcastically, but I still feel like a twat.

Inside, I'm furiously trying to think of something to say. How stupid am I to ask a hot older guy for a lunch date and then not think of anything to say?

'So, Cherry Hinton.' He walks around the bench and stands so close that I have to look up. My whole body feels tingly and I hold my breath. He looks closely at me and I begin to feel awkward. 'I always wondered what Jacob was going on about. You know, he never stops talking about you.'

Surprise loosens my tongue. 'Really? Cos whenever I'm with him he just bangs on about other girls and who he's got to do what to him. Mainly blow jobs...' I tail off awkwardly as this probably is a bit too much information.

'Yeah well, no one wants to act too keen, do they. Got to act a bit hard to get, haven't you?' He flashes me the grin again. He's tall and broad and tanned. He's nearly eighteen and will be out of here in around twelve weeks. It's like I'm talking to a proper grown-up man. I'm still trying to process what he's just suggested. Why would Jacob be playing hard to get, with me?

'I don't believe in playing games. I'm sure if Jacob was into me, he'd just say so.'

'Really? So, this isn't about Jacob, then?'

'What do you mean?'

'You're not here because you're trying to make Jacob jealous or something?'

'No, I'm not some kind of... player. I'm not interested in Jacob because he's not interested in me and if I was into Jacob, I'd ask him to meet me for a lunch date and not you.'

A slow, lazy smile spreads across his face and he reaches down to stroke my neck. I let out a sort of ugly, involuntary whine like a dog desperate for his owner's leftovers and then he's kissing me. It's not my first kiss – that was Kenny Thorpe – but it's the first one that gives me an out-of-body experience and that makes me feel white-hot tingles in my groin.

Then, his hands are up my shirt and he's squeezing my boobs. Then, there is a bang behind us. Felix drops his hands and almost pushes me away. It's Mr Hodson, the head of sixth form. I turn, red and sickened, towards him. He looks from one of us to the other and takes in my untucked shirt, Felix's bulging erection and my messy hair. He scowls in disgust and my stomach turns over with fear.

'I don't want to know what either of you were doing.'

Felix protests, 'Sir, we were just—'

He raises his hand. 'No. Did I or did I not just say that I did not want to know what you were doing or are you deaf as well as extremely foolish?'

Felix runs his hands through his hair and looks very much like an abashed schoolboy. I say nothing and look at the floor.

'Miss Hinton?'

My head shoots up; I can't believe he knows my name. 'Yes, sir?'

'What year are you in?'

'Year Eleven, sir.'

'You haven't aged two years since the start of the day?'

'No, sir.'

Felix tries to have another go. 'Sir, we were just—'

'Mr Stow, I strongly suggest you either continue with the DT project that was so pressing you needed to spend lunchtime completing it, or you leave. You have behaved in a totally inappropriate way – both of you. You know that intense and

prolonged physical contact is not permitted in this school, you know that it is a sixth form privilege to use these rooms at lunchtime and you know, Felix, that you are expressly forbidden from conducting relationships with students who are not in sixth form. And yet, Miss Hinton and you seem to think that the rules don't apply, that you are special, maybe?'

'No, sir,' I say in a strangled voice.

'Maybe,' he continues, sneering at us, 'you think you're Shenfield's version of Romeo and Juliet. Is that it?'

'No, sir.' I can feel hot tears burning my eyes and the back of my throat. 'I'm really sorry.'

He scowls at us both again and holds the door open. 'If ever you disturb our DT block again, your lives shall pay the forfeit of the peace.'

Felix looks at him, totally confused. I walk through the door and can't resist calling to Felix, 'You kiss by the book.'

I swear I see Hodson smile a bit.

'Yeah, course I know Felix. We went to school together. He was loads older than me though. He's an MP, isn't he?'

I always looked back on that incident with mixed feelings. It wasn't like he did anything wrong; I mean, I fancied him loads and I'd asked him for a date. I always felt really ashamed. In an additional awkward twist, it seemed that he'd never told Jacob about it.

Of course, I'd seen him around over the years and I'm sure with his well-reported playboy lifestyle, he didn't even remember my amateurish seduction and subsequent departure. I was sure he'd not ever been short of enthusiastic lovers. He graced the pages of *Hello!* magazine with his arm around various society beauties, each one getting progressively more classy and suitable until the ultimate

MP's wife, Elizabeth Farley-Igglesdon, had been found on a lads' rugby tour of Yorkshire. She had a high-class party shop like a small-scale Carole Middleton and he'd liked her posh accent, private-girls'-school enthusiasm and her commitment to reducing plastic. After he'd bought around £500-worth of bamboo plates and paper straws, she finally gave in and sixth months later *Hello!* was doing a twelve-page spread on their newly refurbished eight-bed pad on Hutton Mount and she'd become plain old Liz Stow.

Interesting then that he'd chosen now to appear on *The Dance is Right*. Chris, of course, had his own view on the matter when I said, 'Isn't the whole thing a bit, er, lightweight for a serving MP?'

'Well, it's all this Europe stuff, isn't it? I mean, of all places, Brentwood is a Tory safe seat but you've got to wonder, how safe is it? Maybe he needs to remind everyone that he's an Essex man through and through – despite the posh northern bird.'

'I guess so. He might be worth having a chat with about all this stuff with Nadiya.'

'Yeah, he would be if you were interested in that sort of thing. If you were going to look into this case for me…'

He smiled his smug greasy smile. He knew he had me; I'd told him as much at the start.

'How much are you going to pay me? It'll mean time away from the shop.'

'I've heard you've got an assistant.'

'Bloody hell, news travels fast. Yes, I've got an assistant who needs paying too. How much, Chris? She's your star. You don't want another Kenny Thorpe on your hands, do you? One live murder on TV is unfortunate, two is the Expose curse…'

He fingered his phone and pretended to think.

'And don't make me play silly games, Chris. You pay me fairly and I'll get this sorted and if there is a story worth telling, I'll make it a good one.'

The special episode of *You're Nicked* in which I revealed who'd killed Kenny Thorpe had become the most watched programme of the 2010s, eclipsing even the original live show of Kenny being murdered. Chris knew I was good at my job.

'Fine. I'll give you £10,000 as a flat fee to keep her safe until the end of the season and find out who's doing this. £5,000 now and £5,000 at the end of the season. If she dies, you don't get the money. If it's a good story with a programme I can make, you get an extra £2,000 bonus.'

He clearly had no idea what the rates on the shop alone were.

'Yeah, nice try, Chris. Let's say we double each of those amounts and you cover my expenses, then maybe we have a deal.'

'Cherry, darling, are you trying to ruin me or what?'

'It's your flagship Saturday night show, Chris. People love it. Even I love it and I hate Expose programmes. Are you prepared for it to go tits up?'

He sighed, scrubbed his hair, scratched his belly, rubbed his hands up and down his trousers, exhaled a few times and then put his hand out. Feeling sick, I shook it. We had a deal.

Chapter Four

Hinton Investigates

By Julia Scofield

It seems that the lure of budget television is always too great for Cherry Hinton. After a scary series of unfortunate events, Chris Gordon has pulled out the big guns and hired Hinton to protect his super sexy star Nadiya Slipchenko while she appears on Expose's flagship Saturday night entertainment show, The Dance is Right. *No stranger to appearing on controversial television herself, Hinton first hit the headlines after appearing on* The Caravan of Love, *where she cavorted with Mark Byrne prior to being kicked off for cheating, an incident which she later claimed was an alleged undercover investigation. Hopefully she'll be in investigative mode when on the set as tensions and passions will be running high backstage as the show begins rehearsals ahead of its gripping fourth live show in what promises to be a thrilling 'luggage week'.*

'Jesus, Cherry, will that woman ever stop reminding people about that flipping caravan programme? Honestly, you must be able to do her for like defamation or something. Such a bitch.' Kelsey was in her usual spot at my counter with the *Essex Chronicle* open, taking up most of the space. In the tiny square of counter I had left, I was decorating some Raspberry Writtle Flapjacks with white chocolate drizzle.

Had I known that the snap some pap had taken of me being escorted out of the caravan on the night of my exposure was to pursue me through the rest of my life, I would have worn a longer T-shirt. There it was again, helpfully placed next to a shot of Nadiya looking glamorous and stunning – I was sure Julia had done it on purpose for maximum shaming effect. Me, dishevelled with no pants or bra, just a T-shirt; Nadiya, statuesque in a ballgown.

'Wasn't it Oscar Wilde who said something about all publicity being good publicity?'

'Is he some like old man influencer or something?' Kelsey replied. 'Bad publicity is bad publicity. Anyways, I think it was P.T. Barnum.'

I stopped what I was doing and gaped at Kelsey. '*P.T. Barnum?*'

'Yeah, circus promotor, they made that film about him.'

'*I* know who he is but more's the point, how do *you* know who he is?'

Kelsey flicked me a disdainful look. 'I do know stuff, you know. I might just do nails for a living but I'm not stupid.'

'I wasn't saying that you were. You know loads of stuff just not, always, you know, boring factual stuff.'

Kelsey pouted a bit and pretended to study the photo of Nadiya. 'Yeah, well, don't judge a book by its cover.' She turned the page and there was a double spread on *The Dance is Right* with a line-up of all the celebrities taking part. I saw her attention was taken up by one participant in particular.

'Kels, is that Joe Rose the host of that quiz programme *Answer This Question* you're looking at there?'

'No.'

'You are, you totally are. Kels, have you been learning facts to impress him on the off-chance that you may meet him as part of my investigation?'

'What? No way?' She pouted some more. 'Well… maybe just a bit. I wanted to be prepared just in case I happened to bump into him backstage or something. How are you so good at knowing stuff like that?'

I laughed and offered her a flapjack that I'd mucked up. 'It's my job. It's like me asking why you are good at painting nails and why they don't go all smudged and chipped within twenty minutes – it's what you're good at.'

She looked pleased at this and used her mermaid shimmer nail to gently caress Joe Rose's photograph. 'Anyways, is old slagbag Scofield right? Have you agreed to do it?'

'Yep, Chris was prepared to pay me for it – I've basically just got to keep her alive for another six weeks. I've chatted to D'arcy, who's fine to do the shop. Mum and Dad are going to do the trad stuff like the London Cheesecakes, Cheese-and-Basildon Scones and that, and D'arcy is going to do the cupcakes and Prosecco pops – things Mum reckons aren't real cakes. So, I'm totally free apart from Ryan and Leigh's dog wellness centre opening cake.'

'Oh is that that Health and Hounds place down William Hunter Way?'

'Yeah, they bought out K9 Fashions from Boughton and decided that there was more money to be made in complementary dog medicine than Barbour Labrador accessories. As you do.'

She folded up the paper and scattered loads of crumbs on the floor as she did so. 'So, what's our next move?'

'I'm going to go and meet everyone on Thursday evening because they'll all be in rehearsing. And I might need someone to make notes for me – if you know anyone who might be free then.'

Kelsey gave me a big hug and a proper kiss on the cheek. 'I am totally gonna be the best assistant you've ever had. Wait until my followers hear about this. I'm gonna break the 'gram.' With that promise lingering in the air along with her latest perfume discovery, Diva d'Essex, she left me to it.

I quickly swept the floor in case a customer who actually wanted to buy some cake came in and put my now complete flapjacks in the window. I checked my list and started the meringue for my Witham Meringue Pie. I felt a nice sense of contentment as I turned over in my head the reasons people might have for wanting to hurt Nadiya. I was lost in a world of spies and dance rivalry when Jacob Stow walked in. It wasn't the first time I regretted not having a job where I had an office that people couldn't just walk into when they felt like it.

Jacob was the hot star of the now cancelled show *You're Nicked*, and when he wasn't busy being hot and famous, he was a DS for the Essex police force. After my last big investigating job, I'd agreed to tentatively start dating him. We had a lot of history; I fancied him like mad but I also knew he was a fickle two-timer with a thing for skinny blondes, hence my reluctance to dive in. I felt that I'd made a really mature decision to just 'date' – it made me feel like a worldly woman who was keeping her options open. At least that's what I told Kelsey when she demanded answers.

'Morning, babe. You alright?' I walked to the back of the shop and flicked the kettle on. 'Want a stale Ingatescone?'

'No thanks, you're alright.' He sounded pissed off.

'You OK, love?'

'Yeah. I'm fine. You?'

I didn't do passive aggression. I'd hoped that after fifteen years of being friends he'd know that. 'What's happened?'

'Nothing.' He picked up a perfectly saleable Sugar Hut Doughnut from a tray in the window and took a bite. Sugar and crumbs shot everywhere.

'Here, at least use a napkin.'

'Who are you? My mum?' he snapped as he snatched the proffered napkin out of my hand.

'Jacob, I can't be doing with this. You've obviously come in for a reason and I haven't got time to play Guess What's Pissing Off Jacob Today. So you can either spit it out or take that stolen doughnut and come back when you're ready to act like a normal person. Your choice.'

He scowled and replied, 'You're doing *The Dance is Right*.'

I knew it. 'Yes, I'm looking after Nadiya Slipchenko while she is on *The Dance is Right*. Is there a problem with that?'

'No,' he said sullenly.

'Good. I'm not investigating anything. I'm just making sure she doesn't have anything else drop on her head.'

'You know who she's dancing with, don't you?'

Ah, now we were getting to the point. 'Yes, she's dancing with Felix. I can't believe you didn't mention that he was going to be on it when I told you how much I enjoy that show.'

'Have you seen him, then?'

'No, not yet. Do you want me to pass on a message? Hasn't he been to see you, then?'

32

Jacob took another big bite of his doughnut and shook his head. 'No, apparently he's too busy with the show. I don't mind about me but it's not fair on Mum. We haven't seen him since the wedding.'

'I'm sorry to hear that. Do you want me to say something if I see him?'

'NO!' Jacob shouted, spraying crumbs and spit in my face. 'I don't want you to go anywhere near him.'

'What?'

'Look at this that he sent me this morning.'

It was a DM starring my terrible picture and beneath it he had written, *You're a lucky man, Jacob, looking forward to getting a slice of the Cherry action for myself!*

A little bit of bile rose up, hot and burning in my throat. 'That's ridiculous. What does he even mean?'

'You fancied him!' The accusation shot out of nowhere.

'Yeah, when I was like fifteen. Everyone did. He was cool and older and the best Danny Zuko since John Travolta. It doesn't mean anything now, does it? He's like some old politician with a prim and proper wife.'

'So why does he think he's going to get some action? Has he been in touch with you?'

I didn't like the tone this conversation was taking. I felt like Jacob was accusing me of giving his sleazy brother some sort of come-on. Fair enough in 2008, but not now. If anything, I wanted to do all I could to avoid Felix. To be honest, I was shocked that he'd even remembered who I was, let alone know that he could wind his brother up through me. And to think I'd been worried that Jacob would be annoyed that I was looking into the accidents on the show.

'Jacob, nothing has happened. The last time I saw Felix was the day he left school. He was stark naked and it took

Hodson, Gould and Madge to get him down off the roof of the sixth form centre. My last view of him was being swathed in Madge's academic gown while he threw up to cheers from the entire school. It was hardly a sexually charged moment that would leave us both clinging on to memories for the next twelve years!'

Jacob shrugged and finished his mouthful. 'I suppose so. Sorry.'

I wasn't terribly impressed by his display of weird jealousy. Particularly how quick he'd been to imply that I was somehow to blame for Felix's pervy attitude towards me. I knew I was right to trust my instincts in not getting over-invested in Jacob. I liked him a lot but I couldn't see myself in a long-term relationship with a guy who found this sort of exchange acceptable and then expected me to totally forget it and get on with things. My feelings for Jacob confused me; I wanted to be with him but, somewhere deep down, I knew that I would never be happy or relaxed with him. I couldn't envisage us growing old and dividing up tedious household chores. It wasn't worth going into right now, though. 'Right. Well, now we've got that sorted, are we going out anywhere tonight?'

He smiled and seemed to revive himself. 'I can't make it tonight; I've got a family thing on. I'm free tomorrow night, though. I thought we could try out that new Mexican-Italian fusion place, Bella Chiquita. According to Ben and Audrey, they do a great four-bean pizza.'

It didn't sound like the most successful marriage of cuisines but at least he was being normal. I made a mental note to do all I could to avoid Felix Stow and accepted Jacob's invite. Apparently, I hadn't lived until I sampled a Bolognese taco!

Chapter Five

Kelsey and I both got the giggles as the security guard waved us through the barrier at Expose's main studio. While I had been here before for my appearance on their lunchtime magazine show, *Mouthy and Menopausal*, and that time when I had filmed my *You're Nicked* special, I hadn't been as excited as I was now.

Kelsey and I were both massive fans of *The Dance is Right* and had watched the previous two seasons with almost religious fervour. Critics had pointed out that the combination of dancing and guessing the cost of household items was not a natural partnership but Chris Gordon, for all his greasy ignorance, knew how to make programmes that people wanted to watch.

Chris had tried to buck the trends followed by dance shows on the major terrestrial channels by making one of the judges just a regular man on the street who spoke 'for the people'. Roy Stone was a legend waiting to be discovered at the age of sixty-four. Out of everyone on the show, it was him I was most excited to meet.

''Ere, do you think that David and Angela Simpson-Timpson will be there tonight? I love it when she gets all emosh and says things like "Oh, my lovely, you truly brought to life the experience of the washing machine…"'

In unison, we chorused, '… you moved me, darling.'

David and Angela were a married couple who owned a now very successful dance school in Southend. They had been regulars on the tea dance and over-thirty-fives circuit before Chris had spotted their potential at a fundraiser at the Cliffs Pavilion and snapped them up for the first season. She oozed cheap Essex glamour and he was twinkly eyed and technical.

I reversed my car into the parking bay that had been reserved for me – a sure sign that Chris was taking his responsibility towards me very seriously. Clearly, Nadiya was a very special asset. Kelsey elbowed me just as I pulled up the handbrake. 'Look over there, in the silver puffa jacket.'

A tiny blonde woman was walking towards the doors clutching a leopard-print coffee cup. Like Nadiya, she moved in a way that appeared to skim the ground rather than make contact with it. Lulu Malone. Lulu was the fourth judge, the only one to have had a truly successful dance career albeit in ballet rather than ballroom. She had retired as the Royal Ballet's prima ballerina aged twenty-six and made most of her income from a YouTube channel in which she demonstrated stretches to help the over sixties beat arthritis. In addition, she sold a range of dancewear that was characterised by being pink with crystal unicorns; Kelsey's little sister, Kaleese, owned most of the collection. Kelsey was on strict instruction to get Kaleese's tracksuit signed tonight or not bother returning home.

We got out of the car and I instructed Kelsey, 'Right, now. Tonight is just about fact-finding, getting a vibe for what's going on and who's who. I'm not going to start asking lots of awkward questions about who's trying to kill Nadiya or anything so your job is to make notes, chat a bit and see if you can pick up on any undercurrents.'

'Undercurrents?'

'Yeah, like, who doesn't like who, who's jealous of so and so. *Do not* spend all evening chatting up Joe Rose.'

Kelsey did her best to look innocent and then gave a sly smile. 'I'll do that if you can manage not to follow Felix Stow round like a rabid dog.'

'What?'

Kelsey snorted. 'Oh come on, Cherry, you well used to fancy him at school. Remember you had that lunch date with him and you came back all red and flustered and wouldn't tell me and Michelle what happened. I don't even know why he said yes in the first place. You were only in Year Eleven and you're loads better-looking now.'

'Thanks for that.' What was it with people reminding me about my very fleeting infatuation with Felix? It wouldn't have been so bad if I wasn't now trying to make it work with Jacob. 'I came back flustered because I made a twat of myself, like I said at the time. Hodson came in and caught us – told Felix to get on with sanding down his picnic bench and told me that unless I'd switched from food tech to resistant materials and aged two years without anyone knowing, I should get out.'

'Right… you know, that would have made you the first girl to have a lunch date with him and not get fingered.'

'Kelsey!' I glanced around the car park to make sure no one could hear this gross conversation.

'Seriously, Kate T. said he was great at it. And she would know!'

'Well, that didn't happen to me. So, er… lucky Kate.' I thought about this for a moment. 'How did he even get her tights and knickers off in public?'

Kelsey had got her phone out and was scrolling through Instagram as we walked towards the entrance. 'She went prepared, didn't she? Lucy had already warned her.'

'That's rank. Why did you let me go in there with my 120-denier tights on, then, if you knew all this?'

Kelsey looked at me with pity. 'No offence but I didn't think he'd bother with you. And like you said, I was right! Anyways, let's go and see if he's improved with age or let himself go.'

I felt sick at the thought of seeing Felix. I almost felt like messaging Jacob and telling him that he really did have nothing to worry about. Felix wasn't interested in me *then* and certainly wouldn't be now.

We were issued with passes at the desk – it was particularly gratifying to be given 'access all areas' green passes. Kelsey instantly took fifteen different shots of hers and started changing the filters. I gave her a look and she responded, 'What? This isn't an undercover mission, is it? We want Nadiya's murderer to know we're on to them.'

A camp, high-pitched voice behind us responded, 'Ooh, darling, you must know something we don't. As far as I know the divine Miss Slipchenko is still with us.'

We turned and came face to face with Miss Gloria Serection and Fanny Batter, a pair of drag queens who hosted the 'green room' section of the show and the spin-off weekday programme, *The Dance is Right – Tonite!* I was a bit scared of them as they seemed to turn everything everyone said into either a cutting put-down or witty innuendo or, if you were really unlucky, both. I went into professional mode.

'Hello, I don't think we've met; I'm Cherry Hinton and this is my friend Kelsey.'

Gloria looked Kelsey up and down before replying, 'I thought for a minute your friend was one of us but then I noticed that she had split ends.'

Fanny guffawed before stage-whispering, 'Gloria, that's not the only split she's got that we haven't.'

Kelsey narrowed her eyes and her lip curled. 'Well, love, at least I actually know how to apply contouring so it makes my face look better instead of looking like I've been punched in both sides of my jaw!'

Fanny and Gloria clutched each other in a parody of being offended. 'Darling,' drawled Gloria, 'you're such a bitch. If you're ever short of a job, you could definitely join us; no one would notice.'

Kelsey opened her mouth to protest again but I pulled her away. 'Kels, leave it. They're just a pair of wind-up merchants.'

'They're a pair of trampy bitches. Did you see those nails? I can't believe they said I could be one of them.'

I shushed her and started dragging her away before they noticed. 'Remember, we're just here for the vibes, not to start anything. OK?'

Her scowl loosened slightly and she nodded. Just in time as Chris barrelled around the corner.

'Ah. Cherry and Kayleigh, was it? Lovely to see you both. Right, I've got a list of everyone who was present on all three occasions with a bit of biog – I thought you might want to start by talking to them, maybe narrow it down a bit but it's totally up to you. As we said, the main job is to be with Nads – make her feel safe, yeah?'

'Right, that's really helpful. Thanks, Chris. Saturday is going to be my first full day with Nadiya and then we'll take it from there.'

'Great, right, well, I'm just going to leave you to it. Do what you like but just keep her alive, yeah?'

And off he went, speaking into his walkie talkie and scratching his bum crack. I studied the list he had given me.

Present at all three incidents:
1. Belinda Price – 26, host of the show, model and face of Corn Chomp, a vegan health cereal.
2. Damien Spiritwind – 48, choreographer and founder of the Spiritwind Foundation for Differently Abled Children.
3. Felix Stow – 31, Conservative MP for Brentwood.
4. Alexi Bondareyev – 32, Ukrainian dancer, World Champion 10 Dances 2018, Nadiya's partner since 2015, possibly in a relationship with Nadiya and / or B. Price.
5. Nic Johnston – 27, band leader and conductor.

Despite the narrowing down of the possible culprits, I still felt it was important to chat to as many people as possible. We followed in the direction that Chris had taken as no one had told us exactly where the studio was. I vaguely remembered the layout from our visit the week before, but all the corridors looked identical. In the distance, I heard a blast of the famous theme tune so I guessed we were on the right track. We got to a large double studio door through which we could see Alexi and his celebrity partner, the glamour model Jodrell Banks, dancing to 'Nellie the Elephant' (I supposed the fact she 'packed her trunk' was enough to meet the luggage theme requirements for this week). We quietly pushed open the doors and tried to slip in unnoticed so as not to disturb the rehearsal.

Unfortunately, Jodrell Banks noticed us immediately and stopped dancing. Jodrell and I had met when she was at rock bottom, having been witness to a murder on a reality show that she was taking part in. She was, at one point, a prime suspect but, after I found the murderer, she and I had become friends and she had demanded that I called her Jodie.

'Fucking hell, look who it is, Cherry Hinton.' She ran over and gave me a massive hug. 'Fuck me, I didn't expect to see you here. What the fuck are you doing here?'

She looked great. Last time I had seen her, she was getting some help for an eating disorder that she'd developed on one of Chris Gordon's previous shows. Clearly, the help was working and she was glowing from the exertion of Alexi's complex dance routine. 'Jodie, you look fab – you look so well. Dancing suits you!'

'Yeah, who'd've thought, eh, Jodie Banks in a leotard. I feel amazing, thanks, babe.'

Alexi had stopped to talk to the band leader, Nic Johnston, and was now sauntering over towards us. He was really fit and really sexy. I could see that Kelsey thought so too. She did a pouty thing with her mouth and kept looking up from under her eyelash extensions. Jodie snaked a possessive arm around his waist and pulled him towards her. His mouth smiled but his blue eyes looked hard and cross.

'Lexi, let me introduce you to a good friend of mine, Cherry Hinton. She's an amazing detective.'

He nodded to me and said, 'Nads tells me that you will look after her. This is true, yes? Chris, he will pay, yes?'

It was hardly small talk but I went along with it. 'Yes, I've come to look after Nadiya and find out what has been going on. You must be really worried about her.'

He shrugged. 'At first, yes, but now, not so much. I think if someone wanted to kill her, then they would. There would not be so many "accidents".'

I was surprised that he wanted to talk about this so openly and right away. I was just preparing my next question when Kelsey piped up, 'Yeah, but what if your aim wasn't so good and that knife had killed her. There would only have been one terrible accident and you would have gone down for murder or manslaughter, surely. It's just bad luck that they keep missing her.'

Alexi shrugged again. 'Most people would say good luck that she was not dead.'

I interrupted, 'Of course, but I think what Kelsey is saying is that I don't think we can dismiss the severity of the problem just because there have been a number of lucky escapes.'

Jodie joined in, 'Yeah, babe, they might just be a very persistent murderer.' She placed her hand lightly on his chest and he batted it away like she was a fly.

'I say they are crap murderer, too many accidents. If I wanted to kill her, I would cut her throat in bed at night, not make a show of it like this.'

He did have a point but it was delivered in such a cold, flat tone that he sounded like a cruel assassin rather than caring lover. I noticed that despite making a display of swatting away Jodie's hand, his left hand was gently caressing her buttocks. I saw Kelsey notice too and we exchanged a look. Before I could say anything, she was in there. 'So, I read in an old magazine that Nadiya was more than just your dance partner, that you were lovers too. Is that still the case?'

He smiled in a way that was calculated to be attractive but which actually looked sinister. Kelsey's pout disappeared and for the first time ever in the presence of a man who wasn't her brother, Kenzee, I saw her look normal.

'When you dance, you are always lovers. The dance floor is the bedroom. The audience are watching you having sex…'

'Tell me about it, babe.' Jodie smirked. This made me laugh a bit too as Jodie had had to resort to having a paying audience watching her do precisely that to make money when we first met.

'They must believe,' he went on, 'that you will go home and make love all night long after the show. But this is an illusion.' He paused momentarily.

Kelsey jumped in, 'Yeah, yeah, I'm hearing you with the old sexy dance stuff but what I'm saying is was you shagging her or not?'

He shrugged and gave up the mystical talk. 'Yes for a while and then no.'

'And now?' I asked.

'Now, not so much.'

Kelsey frowned. 'Is that you being mysterious or just Russian?'

'I am from Ukraine.'

Jodie rolled her eyes. 'For fuck's sake, Lexi, you can tell them. He's shagging me, alright? Not Nadiya, me. I think he's just trying to preserve my honour or something. 'E's such a gentleman. You tell them, Lexi, it's OK.'

He nodded. 'It's true, yes. I am the lover of Jodie.'

I must have looked surprised or something because Jodie said, 'You said yourself how good I was looking. I've even had a boob reduction so Lexi can get really close to me on the dance floor.' She nuzzled his neck and said in a stage whisper, 'Also he's got quite a short willy so it helps with that as well.'

Kelsey's mouth dropped open and I was left speechless.

Only Alexi had anything to say. 'I am also the lover of Belinda Price, who is thinner and easier to do from behind.'

Chapter Six

We all stood there awkwardly looking at one another when we were rescued by Nadiya herself.

'Ah, Cherry, my personal detective and bodyguard. I see you have met Alexi and his latest lover, Jodrell.' She said this last bit with a nasty sneer in her voice.

I replied, 'Yes, *Jodie* is a friend of mine. I'm really pleased that she is having such a good time on the show.'

Nadiya sneered again. 'That is one way of saying it.'

Alexi sneered back and said something that sounded like, 'Yebat tebya, ty chertovski shlyukha!'

Nadiya understood. She flushed red and turned to us. 'Chris, he tells me that he has done some detective work, yes, and has already made a list of the people who were here. I tell you something for free: this man' – she pointed at Alexi – 'would be happy to see me dead.'

Alexi turned away from her and began walking back towards the dance floor; he shouted something and made a universally recognisable gesture. Just so we were all clear.

'Come, let us leave these lovers to "make love on the dance floor",' said Nadiya scornfully.

'That was a well good impression of him,' chirped Kelsey.

'I hear it that many times, it echoes in my head!'

We walked around the edge of the floor where leads, wires and cameras were strewn about. People in black darted around and shouted things like, 'Can we get a close-up of that footwork on camera two, please.' And, 'Alexi, can you make sure she's facing the judges on that turn.' And, 'Nic, love, is it just me or would Beyoncé's "Irreplaceable" not have been a better choice?'

Nic answered back, 'It's only got one sodding box reference. I told Lottie and Tolly, one box reference isn't enough. Unless you've got a better idea, fuck off and let me get on with this. Find me some fucking bag songs!'

Kelsey and I looked at each other and raised our eyebrows. Nic was always portrayed as the mild-mannered, jolly band leader.

Another shout from another person in black: 'Who's doing the *Evita* song, then?'

A voice replied, 'Nads and Felix have got "Another Suitcase in Another Hall" if that's the one you mean?'

More shouting, 'Well, since it's not fucking long-haul-holiday-destination week, I wasn't referring to "Don't Fucking Cry For Me Argentina", was I? You fuckwit!'

We made it round the floor and were now walking towards the judges' desk. Sitting at it in deep conversation were Roy Stone and Lulu Malone. I hissed to Kelsey, 'Quick, get out that tracksuit and Sharpie, this is your moment to get her to sign it.'

Nadiya didn't do the awkward British thing of waiting for them to finish and hovering until they noticed her. She strode up the two steps to the front of the desk and just started to talk at them. 'Roy, Lulu, I wish to introduce my personal safety assistant, Cherry Hinton, and this is her friend.' You can imagine how impressed Kelsey was with that introduction. I'm not sure that I was too keen on 'personal safety assistant' either.

Lulu stood up and there was hardly any change in her height from when she was sitting down. She put out a tiny little perfectly manicured hand and gave me a surprisingly strong handshake. 'Cherry, lovely to meet you. I'm sure I remember seeing you in the summer with that Kenny Thorpe business. You were brilliant.'

I think I was a little bit in love with Lulu. She was so smiley and lovely and small and pink and perfect. 'Thank you very much. I think your dancing is great.' I don't think that I could have sounded more lame if I'd tried.

Lulu smiled again and offered her hand to Kelsey. 'I love your nails, are they snowflakes?'

Kelsey's face lit up with an obsequious smile. 'Yes, yes they are. Because it's winter, innit? Your nails are well nice too.'

Roy coughed a bit. 'Pleased ta meet both you gels too. Be good to see Nads properly looked after. We've all been worried about 'er, int we, Lulu?'

Lulu nodded. 'Oh yes, very worried. It's not right, this is supposed to be a fun family show not a house of horrors.' Her watch beeped and she glanced at it. 'Oh, Roy, you've been sitting still for fifteen minutes, let's do a shoulder stretch, shall we?'

Roy clambered to his feet and let out a sigh with the effort of it all. He rolled his eyes at us. I could see how Lulu's perky loveliness could wear thin for a man like Roy.

Nadiya, too, looked bored by them both and said to me, 'Is there anything you would like to ask them before we move on? There is not much time.'

Kelsey rooted in her bag and pulled put Kaleese's tracksuit top. Lulu was still talking Roy through his stretch, so she hesitated. Nadiya snatched both it and the Sharpie from her. 'I will sign it.'

Before Kelsey could protest, Nadiya had scrawled her signature right across the back of it and shoved it back into Kelsey's hand. Kelsey looked at me aghast and I hurriedly took it off her and shoved it back in my bag.

'I'm sure Kaleese doesn't actually know what Lulu's signature looks like anyway. Don't say anything – please,' I begged quietly.

Nadiya was marching off and we barely had time to say goodbye to Lulu and Roy, who were still stretching. She led us up to a small office at the back where Belinda Price and Jason Devine were running through their scripted lines. I hissed at Kelsey, 'Do not say anything about Alexi or his willy or having it doggy style, OK?'

Kelsey made her face the picture of innocence. 'God, Cherry, as if I would.'

Nadiya opened the door and, with a very fake smile, said, 'Belinda, darling, this is Cherry Hinton. She is a detective. She will discover who has been trying to hurt me.' And then she turned and left us there.

Belinda was all smiles. 'Ah hello, come on in. Chris told us to be expecting you. I'm Belinda Price and this is Jason.'

Jason stood up slightly and shook hands. 'Jason Devine, nice to meet you.' He sat down again, and it became quickly apparent that there was nowhere for me and Kelsey to sit. There was a desk covered in papers, so I opted to lean against it. Kelsey slouched against the door like an ineffectual guard.

I cleared my throat awkwardly. 'Please, carry on; don't let us interrupt.'

Belinda smiled again; she seemed nice. 'OK, well, can you tell us if this sounds a bit desperate or not? Jace and I were just trying to make it sound right.'

He chimed in, 'Yeah, we've got to do a plug for Damien's charity but the script sounds really crass.'

'Don't worry, mate, I'll tell you if it sounds shit or not,' offered Kelsey eagerly.

'OK,' said Belinda. 'Here we go: While we're all here enjoying the dancing and the exquisite luggage provided by our sponsor LS Furnishings, there's some people who are less fortunate than us.'

'Tonight,' continued Jason, 'spare a thought for the other ones, spare a thought when you're having fun, put your arms around the disabled children this Christmas. Do they know it's dancing time at all?'

'It sounds vaguely familiar,' I hazarded. 'Did Damien write it?'

'He writes anything that relates to his charity,' replied Belinda. 'It just sounds a bit trite to us, no matter how you say it.'

'Sounds shit,' said Kelsey. 'You need to just be upfront about it – some kids have got no legs and that and can't dance so give them some money for dead fancy wheelchairs or better prosthetics. Job done.'

Belinda smiled again; she was very good at smiling. Perfect for this job. 'That's really useful input. Thank you both. So, Cherry, you're here to take care of Nads, are you?'

'Yes, that's right. You were here when the first accident happened, weren't you?'

'I was here when all three happened! Looks a bit suspicious, doesn't it?' She pulled a funny face and Jason patted her knee. She reached down and squeezed his hand.

'Well, you weren't the only one. Can you tell me anything about Nadiya, like why anyone would want to hurt her?'

Belinda looked shocked. 'I absolutely haven't got a clue. Nads is, like, so popular. Everyone loves her; she's like everyone's best friend, isn't she, Jace?'

'Yeah, yeah.' He nodded obediently.

She continued, 'She's so much fun and so good at dancing. It's like she's the star of the show. You know, part of me wants to think that those things that happened were just silly accidents. I just can't think who would want to hurt her.' She tilted her head to one side and smiled again to show just how sincerely she believed herself.

Kelsey was having none of it and blurted out before I could stop her, 'That's all well and good but aren't you shagging her ex? He seems to hate her and he threw a sharp knife at her head.'

Belinda swallowed a few times and her smile slipped slightly. 'I don't see… I can't understand… Sorry, I just don't see how that's related. Yes, Alexi and I have… spent time together but surely that would mean she would dislike him and want to hurt him.'

'If he really *has* broken up with her,' said Kelsey, grinning.

Belinda shook her head furiously. 'No, I'm sorry. That is not possible. He has to sleep with that Banks woman – it's in the contract – but he has *chosen* me!'

This was an interesting nugget. 'In the contract? Sex? That seems a bit… odd.'

Belinda turned to me. 'Oh yes, Chris wants the viewers to think that the dancers are shagging their partners – what better way to achieve that than by making it happen? It's only the young and attractive celebrities who must sign the contract. I think they get paid more and obviously they stay in longer. I mean, I think if anyone was really not up for it, they wouldn't force the issue but, you know, it's that sort of environment. People want to have sex with other attractive people.'

I was shocked. I felt like a prudish auntie at a strip club. 'Gosh, well. I never knew that. So is Nads expected to sleep with Felix, then?'

Jason laughed in surprise. 'No, he's very married and it wouldn't look good for an MP to be carrying on like that. Besides Nads likes—'

'Jason,' Belinda interrupted, 'the poor woman is in danger, it's not nice to be gossiping about her.'

He rolled his eyes at us and looked guilty. Damn Belinda and her principles.

Belinda suddenly seemed quite keen to get rid of us. From the window of the office, we could see everyone. I saw Joe Rose, the quiz master of Kelsey's dreams and host of what was possibly the dullest quiz of all time, *Answer This Question*. As a reward for Kelsey not making a fuss about Kaleese's tracksuit, I announced, 'Anyway, lovely to meet you both, we're just going to nip down and chat to a few of the contestants. Is that Joe Rose I see down there?'

Belinda and Jason both smiled and nodded some more. 'Oh yes, Joe, so nice, such a charmer.'

'Amazing dancer and so funny.'

'Yes, such a sense of fun.'

'So charming.'

They were like a weird two-headed positivity beast. We backed away from them down the stairs and headed over to where Joe was sitting looking at his phone. There was no sign of Nadiya and I couldn't see his professional partner, Georgie Fenton, so it seemed like a good opportunity to get him on his own.

'Er, hello. I'm Cherry Hinton. I'm investigating what's been happening to Nadiya.'

He glanced up briefly from his phone, said, 'Right,' and dropped his gaze back to the screen.

I could see Kelsey's lip twitching like she was summoning her customary snarl. I shook my head at her and tried again. 'Look, I'm sorry to bother you, Mr Rose, I just wanted to ask a few questions.'

'Yeah, and maybe you could *answer* them. That would be ironic, then, wouldn't it? You *answering* questions rather than asking them,' said Kelsey, looking pleased with herself.

Joe's head lifted and he looked at her with the same withering, patronising look he used on his show when one of the contestants gave a wrong answer. 'No, it wouldn't be ironic, it would be an amusing play on words that creates a sense of a happy coincidence.'

That told us then. Kelsey looked crushed. Which made me cross. 'Er, Mr Rose, I'm sure whatever it is that you are looking at is vitally important but if you'd like to continue appearing on a show that has a slightly wider fan base than the usual ten nerdy losers who watch your quiz, I suggest that you do all you can to help me. There is a woman's life at stake here.'

'Yeah,' said Kelsey, leaning over his shoulder, 'studying the history of ancient Greek socio-politics ain't gunna help anyone.'

Joe Rose looked up at me totally affronted. 'I sincerely hope that this is worth interrupting me for with your inane chatter. Rumour has it, Cherry Hinton, you're an intelligent woman who is good at this sort of thing. But it doesn't take a genius to know that most rumours only contain a grain of truth,' he concluded with a tight, unconvincing smile.

I couldn't believe that this was the same 'charmer' we'd heard Belinda and Jason gushing over minutes before. 'I only wanted to ask if you had seen or noticed anything unusual when you were in Nadiya's company.' I could see now why his partner, bubbly Welsh newcomer Georgie Fenton, was not spending any time with him outside of compulsory practices – at least that's why I assumed she wasn't waiting with him.

Joe shrugged. 'Everything here is unusual to me. A silly fantasy world where mahogany book cases and dishwashers are more important than knowledge.'

We were rescued from this awkward exchange by Nadiya suddenly appearing on the other side of the dance floor with Felix on her arm. It was time to go and say hello.

My legs shook as we picked our way over the cables and props to the edge of the floor. I was surprised by how nervous I felt about seeing Felix again. They were dancing a waltz to a song from *Evita*. It looked beautiful. When the song finished, Kelsey and I burst into applause. Nadiya looked over and smiled. Felix glanced at us and then did a double take when he realised who we were. He rushed over, beaming.

'Kelsey Scott and Cherry Hinton. How are you lovely ladies?' He gave us each a big hug but I'm sure that mine was longer. 'Long time no see. You both look exactly the same as I remember you.'

'You've got more clothes on than last time I saw you,' I said, trying to be witty but instantly regretting it when I saw a smirking look in his eye.

'Is that right? Which time are you talking about, Cherry?'

Kelsey, oblivious to the slight awkwardness, answered for me. 'When you were on top of the sixth form centre singing "My Way" after your last A level exam. You were naked, remember?'

He threw back his head and laughed poshly like all MPs seemed to do. 'Yes, I remember that. I thought Hodson was going to go blind – his eyes were bulging so far out of his head. He had to get Gould up there to tackle me to the roof. I was totally off my tits. Woke up the next morning and couldn't work out where the gravel burn had come from. Probably thought I'd got lucky in the car park at The Eagle and Child or something.' He laughed again then leant in towards me and murmured urgently, 'Cherry, I've got to talk to you about something. Make an excuse to leave in five minutes. I'll wait outside. Laugh like I've said something sexy and funny.'

I was a bit surprised at this sudden demand but went along with it anyway. I let out a weird high-pitched laugh that I'd seen women like Nadiya do.

Felix turned to Nadiya and said, 'Nads, darling, just had a call from the office. Some garbled message about another vote. Got to go and chase it up. Back in a tick.' He marched off the floor purposefully and looked at me over his shoulder. I checked the time on the studio clock.

Nadiya was showing Kelsey where they had repaired the floor after the hook incident the week before. I turned my attention back to them. 'That must have been so terrifying for you. Did they ever find out what caused it to happen?'

'No, there was supposed to be a bolt that held it in place and when the technician went up there, the bolt had, how do you say, steered? Into two.'

'Sheared.'

'That's it, sheared into two pieces. A solid clump of metal. That doesn't just happen, does it?'

We both nodded and tutted appropriately. Then the alarm on my phone went off. I made a show of looking annoyed and shouted as I ran out of the studio, 'It's an important call, I must take this.' I'm sure that Kelsey knew the difference between an alarm and my ringtone, but I hoped I could rely on her to not say anything.

True to his word, Felix was out in the car park sitting on a bench by the entrance. He glanced up warmly as I approached and patted the seat next to him. I sat down but tried to sit as far away from him as I possibly could. He couldn't help but notice what I was doing.

'Cherry, thank you for coming out. I wouldn't have blamed you if you'd chosen to say inside.'

'You said you wanted to tell me something,' I said, looking ahead into the dark car park.

'I wanted to tell you that I haven't forgotten what happened.'

'Me neither,' I said.

'I'm not proud of who I was at school. I took advantage of being good-looking and popular. I wasn't very nice to girls… to you.'

This was going to be a humiliating non-apology that would end up with him making me say it was all OK and that he'd done nothing wrong. I could tell. He was such a politician. I said nothing.

'Cherry, look at me.'

I turned to face him and still said nothing.

'I knew that you were attracted to me and I used you because I wanted to get one over on Jacob. I wanted to prove to him that there was nothing I couldn't have and that included you. But I just did what I wanted so I could tell Jacob about it later.'

I was incredulous. 'You got off with me just to prove a point? To Jacob?'

'Yes.' He looked down at the floor.

My stomach lurched sideways. 'You didn't fancy me or anything?'

'Not… really. I mean you weren't *unattractive* but… you were in Year Eleven and wore bodyshaper tights. And then, that other time, in Chelmsford, you were just… there.'

'You did those things just to upset your brother?'

'It sounds really bad when you put it like that…'

'That's how you put it, Felix. And yes, you're right, it *does* sound bad. It sounds like a fucking pile of shitty shit, Felix.'

'It was a long time ago. I thought you'd be OK with it…' He was beginning to whine.

'No, actually, I'm not OK with it, Felix. It would have been better if you'd just left it at "sorry" but the fact you were a. not into me in the slightest and b. only did it to upset your perfectly nice brother, who, c. wasn't even interested in me at that point makes me feel like the world's biggest twat.'

'You're wrong,' he said quietly.

I knew it; he was somehow going to make this my fault. 'How am I?'

'He *was* interested. He was *always* interested. You know half the girls and all of the stories were made up. He'd come home each night and tell me about something you'd said in some lesson or another. Ask my advice. I told him to make you jealous, talk about other girls. Actually get off with other girls.'

I couldn't really believe what I was hearing. Sometimes men are dicks. 'That was shit advice. Properly shit.' I spent most of the time thinking he was just a player. By the time I realised he might like me, it was too late.

Felix sat back in the bench and sighed. 'I know. He came home after that night at Matt Shepherd's party and I was like, "What happened? You get your dick wet?" And he was like, "No, she didn't believe me." He had planned to lose his virginity that night and you ran away.'

'Shit.' Like I needed my memory of that horrid night made any worse. 'Felix, I really wish you hadn't told me that. You know what, I wish I'd never come out here at all. You've made everything worse.'

'Sorry,' he said in a small voice. 'I never told him about, you know...'

'The non-consensual assault when I wasn't quite sixteen.'

That got his attention. 'Hang on, let's watch it with the loaded terms, Cherry. You weren't fighting me off, were you? And what about afterwards? When you were older?'

We could easily be here all night and Kelsey would be coming to look for me soon. 'Look, just because you've become an MP doesn't mean you have to turn all sleazy and make excuses for yourself. I always thought that you were alright, you know. Especially after that time in Chelmsford.'

He interrupted, 'About that, all of it I mean. I wanted to talk to you because, well, I'd hate for any of it to, er, be made public now that I'm with Liz.'

'What on earth do you mean?'

'Well, your brand isn't exactly the brand that I would like to be aligned with in the media.'

Was he actually saying what I thought he was? I looked directly at him. 'What brand is that, Felix?'

'Er, you know, that programme you were on, with the caravans. It's just I've got an image to, er, protect.'

Suddenly it became clear that this is what the whole conversation had been about – the newly wed MP wanted to ensure that his association with 'sex-mad nympho Cherry Hinton' (as I had once been called) was not going to find its way into the *Essex Chronicle* or any other media outlet. I was so angry, I could hardly speak. Through a clenched jaw, I managed to say, 'Right now, Jacob and I are slowly working things out. Let's make a deal: you don't ever mention to Jacob what happened and you don't go winding him up or alluding to the fact you may find me attractive—'

He jumped in. 'Which I don't.'

'Alright, Felix, you've made that clear, thanks. And I will not mention myself and your name together in the same breath to anyone. Ever. OK?'

'Yes, that's fine. Thank you, Cherry, I knew you'd understand.' He smiled, hopped up off the bench and bounded back through the studio doors.

I was left with a nasty oily feeling that I'd somehow given Felix exactly what he had come out here for. That I'd played into his hands in some odd, undefined way. The best I could hope for was that he'd be voted off soon.

'Cherry, what you doing?' Kelsey interrupted my thoughts.

I stood up quickly and tried not to look weird or guilty. 'Felix wanted to talk to me. I thought he was going to tell me something useful about Nads but he just wanted to go on about Jacob and me.'

Kelsey shrugged at this; it wasn't a very interesting topic, to be fair, and she clearly had something she wanted to tell me. 'Right, get this. You know how Jason was going to tell us who Nads fancied and Belinda interrupted?'

'Yeah?' I was all ears.

'So I says to Nads, "Cor, I wouldn't mind shagging Felix, bet he is a goer in the bedroom department." And she gives it, "Yeah, he is amazing." And I'm like trying to play it cool and find the undercurrent like you said. So I say, "But hasn't he just got married, though?" and she goes, "Yeah, married men are the best because they don't expect any commitment" and then, you're going to love this, then, she gives it, "Not like Jason, who won't leave me alone."'

'No way!'

'I know I thought he was totally asexual. Just kind of tanned and attractive. Like a Ken doll.'

My mind was spinning. Was there *anyone* on this programme who wasn't sleeping with someone else on the show? A wave of tiredness – maybe from sitting in the cold and dark for so long – swept over me. I turned to Kelsey, who was tapping away on her phone. 'I've had enough of this for one night; do you want to go The Crystal Lounge for a drink?' I thought we ought to make the most of not being fully 'on duty' until Saturday morning.

She looked up eagerly. 'Yeah sure, let me just update my location. I'll be right with you. My followers are going to be well impressed. I've just left the set of *The Dance is Right* and now I'm off to a top Brentwood night spot. It's hard being so busy and popular.'

'Popular? You've been everywhere with me!'

'Well, they don't need to know that bit, do they? It's all about the overall lifestyle, isn't it? I need to project the right image. Anyways, your social currency is riding high – you solved a crime and now you're protecting Nadiya Slipchenko. For once, you're making me look good rather than viser verser.'

'Vice versa.'

'Whatevs, Cherry, no one likes a pendant!'

Chapter Seven

The Crystal Lounge was having a two-for-one on cocktails so, despite it being a Thursday, the place was heaving. We wove ourselves through the crowds to the bar and waited to catch someone's attention. I was in the mood for an almond Baileys. I didn't bother asking Kelsey what she wanted as she only ever drank the same thing in here – Passoã and lemonade. I was sure that she was the only person in the whole of Brentwood who drank the stuff as they always had to fish the bottle out from the back of the baroque bar display.

We finally got served and we dragged ourselves back through the crowd to the courtyard, which was relatively empty and mainly occupied by vapers and old-school smokers.

'God, I thought I'd never be able to breathe properly again. Can't believe how busy it is on a Thursday,' I said as I put my drink down and slid onto the bench.

'Thursday is the new Saturday,' said Kelsey sagely. 'It's programmes like *The Dance is Right*, keeping people in.' She took a big mouthful of her pink, passion-fruit-flavoured drink and smacked her lips like it was some vintage whiskey or something.

I took advantage of her silence. 'Right, let's just go over what we both noticed tonight and check where we're at with everything.'

'OK, Sherlock! I made notes on my phone, well, not notes as such, more like pictures.'

'Kels, did you take pictures with your phone?'

'Yeah. That.'

I supressed a sigh. She wasn't the best sidekick in the world but she was good fun and often said the things that I wouldn't dare to.

'OK, so do we think that there is a crime here? Is Nadiya in danger or is she imagining it?'

Kelsey pondered this for a moment and took her hand off her phone, which was always a sign of deep thought on her part. 'I'm gonna say yeah. I think *one* of those things happening – the wrong knife in Alexi's costume, the camera running away onto the dance floor, the hook falling down – that could be an accident, but all three in three weeks? I'm not buying it.'

'I agree. OK, so Chris made us a handy list of people who were there when all three happened. Do we need to look outside of the list?'

'Who's on it again?'

I ticked them off on my fingers. 'Belinda Price, Alexi Bondareyev, Damien Spiritwind, Nic Johnston and Felix. I think the knife could have been set up beforehand.'

Kelsey frowned. 'Yeah, the knife deffo but the camera and the hook were all about timing – the murderer needed to make them happen at the right time and they couldn't know in advance where Nadiya would be.'

She was right. This helpfully narrowed the pool of suspects to Chris's list unless we were looking for more than one person. 'So, what do we know about Alexi; why would he want to kill Nadiya?'

'It's like he doesn't like her but he's moved on – she's not stopping him from sleeping with whoever...'

'Yeah and he's still competing at an international level without her. You're right, she's not holding him back or anything. It's like Belinda said, Nadiya's got more reason to want him dead than the other way around.'

I paused and took a sip of my drink. I wasn't sure I entirely liked it but it was too busy to go and get another one.

'OK, so what about Felix, then?'

'Well, he might not want it to get out that he's been sleeping with her. That would screw up his marriage and being an MP and that but I can't see it.'

I knew what she meant. I couldn't imagine him sneaking around, cutting metal bolts in half and switching knives in costumes. If Felix was going to commit a murder, I saw him as the sort of person who'd hire someone else to do a hit and run or something. A useless coward.

'Out of the people we met, I'd say it was that Belinda.' Kelsey banged her glass down emphatically.

'Why? Is it because you didn't like her?'

'Yeah! She did too much smiling. No one real smiles that much.'

'But there's still no reason for her to want to kill Nadiya,' I reasoned. 'Yes, she's seeing Alexi but like we just agreed, Nadiya isn't standing in the way of that. Nadiya's dancing gives Belinda a show to host. Just because she's annoying and unlikeable doesn't mean she's a would-be murderer.'

'Have you seen her Instagram?' asked Kelsey as she unlocked her phone absently.

'Not yet, no.'

'She does those wanky pictures of like some basic mug, some leaves and a blanket from somewhere posey with some lame caption like, "Getting all fucking cosy now it's cold. Use my code to get money off a shit mug like mine from some shit over-priced shop for people with no design ideas of their own." Here.' She showed me.

I laughed; I hated that kind of stuff too. 'Does she also do photos of herself where her top half is facing the front and her bottom half is facing sideways and she's wearing some cheap-looking dress from one of them catalogues…'

'Yeah one of them catalogues where you know someone like Belinda Price would never shop from and she's got a caption like, "Feeling fine today in this chunky knit from cheapo shit clothes catalogue, here use my code to get a quid off but you'll never look as nice as I do because you haven't got a personal trainer, chef and stylist."'

We cackled with laughter and I snorted a bit of my drink out of my nose.

I rummaged in my bag for a tissue and wiped my face. 'Then there's Damien and Nic.'

'Yeah, I'd forgotten about them. This is pretty hard, Cherry. No one has a reason for wanting Nadiya dead.'

'Ah, well, that's what they want us to think. Yes, on the surface everyone is either shagging her or over it but it's my job to find out what they are hiding. This is just the beginning, Kels.'

There was clearly a lot that we were missing. While I tried to sound confident to Kelsey, I did feel a lot like I was stabbing in the dark. I thought that my next move needed to be a meeting with Damien, preferably before Saturday when I would be watching over Nadiya all day. We sipped the remainder of our drinks in silence when I heard a familiar laugh from the corner of the yard. I slipped out from the table and walked over to where I heard the laugh.

'Alright, Cherry.' A voice came out of the gloom.

'Jacob?'

'What are you doing here?'

'That's not the best greeting I've ever had.' Then I saw that he was not alone. He was with a woman I'd never seen before.

'Sorry, I was just, er, surprised. You said you were at the studio tonight. I didn't expect to see you here.'

'Clearly. Are you going to introduce me?' I shot daggers at the simpering woman on the other side of the table.

He coughed and rearranged his hair. 'Yes of course, Cherry, this is Liz – my sister-in-law. Liz, this is Cherry—'

Kelsey interrupted, 'His girlfriend.'

Jacob's eyebrows shot up quizzically and I pulled my best nonchalant face. 'Hi, Liz, nice to meet you. I saw Felix earlier; his dancing is coming on well.' I put out my hand to shake hers.

She leant across the table and gave my hand a hearty shake. I noticed that she was wearing what appeared to be a fleece and some sort of utility-style trousers. I instantly stopped being suspicious at that point. She picked up a pint glass, which I had assumed was Jacob's, and drained the contents. I decided that I liked her. Kelsey and I carried on standing there until Jacob got over himself and invited us to join them. He squeezed my waist and told me I looked lovely. The three of us sent him to the bar to replenish the drinks.

Liz turned to us both and said conspiratorially, 'This is m' first time in Brentwood. I don't think I'm wearing the right clothes. I said to our Jacob, what should I wear like for a night'on'town and 'e says "Summat comfy." I look like a local tramp.'

Kelsey scrutinised her. 'To be fair, the local tramp has a few more labels going on. I mean, Berghaus might be big in Yorkshire where you actually get full-on avalanches and stuff but here, outdoor wear is more…'

'More faux fur and less Gore-Tex,' I agreed.

'Right.' Liz nodded. 'I was dead nervous cos I hadn't met any of the Stows properly. They were at the wedding but I didn't really chat to Felix's family. Spent most of the time having us photo took. Then I got shit-faced and spent the rest of the night on the dance floor.'

'Sounds like a perfect wedding!' I said.

'Felix went mad cos I passed out on the bed. I'd spent a fortune on fancy underwear for the big night but was so pissed I didn't have clue what was going on. I didn't see him again until the morning. He'd spent the night in the best man's room.'

Kelsey and I exchanged a look before offering expressions of sympathy.

'So yous two went to school with Felix?'

'Yeah,' I replied, 'he was a few years older than us, which, when you're fifteen and eighteen, is massive. He was a bit of a legend.'

'Oh aye?'

'Yeah,' said Kelsey. I prayed that she wasn't going to say anything about the lunch dates. 'He played Danny Zuko in *Grease*. I won't tell a lie, all the girls thought he was well fit. In fact, he paraded naked on the roof on the day of his last exam. It took three teachers to get him down.'

'Aye, that sounds about right. He's such a show-off. That's why he's doing so well on *The Dance is Right*.'

Jacob came back with the drinks and chatted to me while Kelsey and Liz discussed Felix's chances of winning the show. 'I'm sorry I didn't say I was coming out.'

I shrugged it off. 'Don't be silly, I'm not your keeper. You can do what you want.'

He smiled. Although he was annoying and bossy most of the time, that smile could always keep me coming back for more. 'And now you're my girlfriend?'

I felt a bit shy suddenly. 'Yeah, if you like.'

'I do like. I like very much indeed. I like so much I'm gonna take you home with me.'

I giggled and felt all coy and silly. 'Good. I'd like that. Um, what about Liz?'

'Oh, don't worry about her.' He glanced at his watch. 'Felix should be here soon to pick her up. They're staying at Marygreen Manor.'

I wished that Felix wasn't coming but there wasn't much I could do about it and besides, I needed to get used to seeing him about if I was going to help Nadiya.

We were all having a good laugh at a story Jacob was telling about when he and Felix were little and Felix had got his arm stuck in a vending machine at Shenfield station when Felix turned up.

'Evening all. Cherry, Kelsey – fancy seeing you two here. Can't seem to get rid of you now.' We laughed weakly. 'What the fuck are you wearing, Liz?'

Any mirth was instantly sucked out of the moment and we all looked at him awkwardly. Liz tugged apologetically at the sleeves of her fleece and her eyes filled with tears.

I spoke up. 'Well, that's one way of greeting your new wife…'

Kelsey joined in. 'Maybe they haven't caught up in the north yet but we tend to say "Hello, love, were you OK while I went off dancing with red-hot Russians?" or, you know, something like that.'

Felix ignored us both and looked Liz up and down. 'What happened to the dress I put out for you to wear, eh?'

'Actually, mate, that was my fault; I got to the hotel to pick her up and I said we weren't going anywhere fancy and just to put something warm on so she got changed,' said Jacob.

Felix didn't reply to any of us. He looked at Liz and said, 'Next time, you wear what I tell you to. You're my wife and you're in my constituency now. I don't expect to find you dressed up like you're going for a fucking hike. Let's go.'

Liz finished the last of her drink and weakly said goodbye. Kelsey checked her phone and said she'd better be heading off too. Which left me and Jacob.

'Have you got your car?' I asked, suddenly conscious of the practicalities of going back to Jacob's house. And what that actually meant.

'Nah, I walked up from the station. How many drinks have you had?'

'Only a Baileys, Officer. I've only had mouthful of this one.' I indicated the drink he'd just bought.

'Right, well, leave that. You need to come with me on an urgent police matter.' He smiled again and my legs barely held me up.

I knew that Kelsey would want a detailed account of what Jacob's flat looked like and the order of events but I don't really remember how we got there or how we got from the front door to his bedroom.

We were kissing and taking our clothes off and I truly did want to savour the moment but I also wanted to get there, I wanted to actually have sex with Jacob. He tried to slow me down and be a gentleman. A number of times he asked if I was sure, if everything was OK. Finally, in a strangled voice, I pulled his head towards mine and whispered, 'Just fuck me.' And he did. Repeatedly. In every conceivable way and in some ways I'd never thought of before. I was a moaning, quivering mess by the time we were done.

I woke up to find an empty flat and a note which promised a repeat performance after our date at Bella Chiquita that evening. With stiff legs and aching arms, I took a shower and came out smelling of bergamot, sandalwood and masculinity. I staggered around hunting for my knickers and socks and finally got dressed in my clothes from the night before.

My one aim for the day was to hunt down either Damien Spiritwind or Nic Johnston. I was fairly confident that either one or both would be at the studio but I was hoping to see them away from that environment. There was something about that accident-prone set which made me feel uneasy.

Chapter Eight

I called Chris as I brushed my hair and reapplied a bit of lip balm. He forwarded me Damien's contact details and by the time I was ready to leave Jacob's place, I'd arranged to meet him at his dance school on an industrial estate in Hutton. Just around the corner from my mum and dad's place. I calculated that I could meet him for a chat and then drop home for a cup of tea and a wee before I went back to the shop to check everything was OK with D'arcy. I loved it when a plan came together. Life was good that morning.

After a few wrong turns and a long conversation with a tyre repair man, I finally found the Spiritwind School of Dance. It didn't look much from the outside – just another anonymous industrial building – but inside was a world of mirrors, fancy lighting and a beautiful sprung wooden floor. A display case by the front door was laden with trophies and medals won by students at the school. This Damien obviously knew what he was doing. No sooner had I stepped through the door, I heard him talking on the phone in his office.

'Jackie, darling, tell Children in Need that we'll be absolutely honoured to put something together for them. I'm not going to go with what they brought to the table, though.

I just don't think differently abled children should be used that way. What I want to do, though, is create something that fuses together the joy of movement with the paralysis of the soul. The inner toddler versus the aged body?'

He paused and I held my breath, eager to hear what Jackie thought of his ideas.

'No, no, no, you're not listening. I don't want to use differently abled children for this – it's simply too on the nose darling. I want to capture the sense of being differently abled without being crass.'

He paused again.

'Jackie, sweetie, listen. No wheelchairs. No amputees. The spirit but not the actuality. No… that's not… no terminally ill children! For God's sake, woman, it's supposed to be an entertainment show. Oh fuck off!'

I tiptoed back to the front door and opened and closed it vigorously. He appeared in the doorway and was the absolute opposite of what I expected. He was bulging with muscles beneath a tight white T-shirt and wore ripped jeans with a massive belt buckle. His biceps, forearms and shoulders were a mass of tattoos, all jostling for space. He said, 'Hi, you must be Cherry,' and held out his hand.

Surprised, I said, 'Yes, that's me. Thank you for fitting me in.'

He showed me into his office, which was a neat, well-ordered space and could have belonged to the owner of any successful business. I sat down in the chair he indicated and declined a hot drink. He sat opposite me and said, 'Right, what can I do to help?' in what was a very different voice to the one he'd just used on the phone. Obviously, I didn't comment on it.

'So, I'm here to ask about Nadiya Slipchenko. I assume you know what's been going on with the, er, accidents…'

'Indeed.'

'So, were you there when the first one happened?'

'Yes.' Clearly not a chatty man.

'Can you talk me through what happened?'

'Do I need a lawyer?'

'Well, since I'm not the police, I wouldn't have thought so but it's up to you, mate.'

He looked at me speculatively. 'What exactly are you doing, Cherry?'

'Well, the main thing I'm doing is making Nadiya feel better so she still wants to go out and dance on Saturday. Pretty crucial for a dance show, I'd say.'

'And what's in it for you?' Where had the airy-fairy jazz-hands guy gone?

'The management are paying me.'

He laughed. 'I assume you have other forms of income, Cherry. Seriously, though, what's in it for you?'

I sighed. 'A story, maybe. Getting to hang out with the delightful stars of the show like you.' I gave him a sarcastic smile.

He grinned back. 'Right, well now we're clear we can get on, can't we?'

'You aren't like what I expected.'

'Really?'

'When you're on *The Dance is Right – Tonite* with Fanny Batter and the other one, you seem more, er…' I fumbled for the right word that didn't sound offensive.

'Camp? Over the top? more *Damien Spiritwind*?'

'Yeah, like that.'

He leant back in his chair and waved his arm around the office to illustrate what he said. 'All of this, the awards, the office, the studio, the business – they are the result of Mike Foster's hard work.'

'Who is…'

'I am Mike Foster; Damien Spiritwind is my alter ego.'

'Like Lady Gaga – without the meat, obviously.' Great way to handle a tricky interview, Cherry.

'It's all my ideas; I'm a brilliant dance teacher but Damien Spiritwind is what people want, what people expect – I'm just giving them the magic, the sparkle, the mysticism of the dance.'

'Ri… ight, the mysticism of the dance.' To be fair he did have a point.

'So, that's me. I'm not some razzmatazz spirit-fingered dance wizard; I'm a normal guy who runs a successful business. Don't try to trick me because it won't work.'

He seemed quite paranoid and defensive. I wondered why. 'I take it you haven't had good experiences in the past.'

'Not with Nadiya Slipchenko at any rate.'

'Meaning?' He really was hard work.

'She tried to sue me when she found out she couldn't compete any more.'

'Why?' I wasn't going to make it round to Mum and Dad's at this rate. I was usually better than this at getting people to talk to me. Maybe I needed to take a leaf out of Kelsey's book and use provocative tactics to get him saying more.

'She was part of this dance school when she first arrived from Russia in 2006. She had some sort of injury in her lower leg but it was OK and she was very successful but then, suddenly, it's not OK and after the World Ballroom Championships in 2016 she could hardly walk. Then, despite all of the support we had given her, the hours of tuition and the space to work, we get a letter from her solicitor saying that we had not taught her correctly, that the leg injury had been made worse by our teaching and she was claiming a loss of earnings from us. Millions of pounds.'

'Oh my God, that's terrible. Why would she do that?'

'Because she's a manipulative evil bitch. That's why.'

'So, what happened?' At last, someone with a reason to dislike Nadiya.

'We fought it, proved that she had known about the injury and what would happen if she continued dancing on it. Proved that we had taken the right amount of precautionary action and advised her correctly. Blew her stupid case out of the water. She just wanted a load of money and saw us, my wife and I, as an easy target.'

'That's horrible. How do you cope with working with her now? It must make choreographing group dances on the show really tricky.'

He shrugged. 'When I am Damien Spiritwind, nothing can touch me.' He changed his voice to Damien's. 'It's about the movement of spirit through space. We are not individuals, we are a collective of spirits moving through time and space, creating a thing of beauty. There is no time to be you and me, just one being moving together of one accord.'

I tried hard not to laugh. He was kind of laughing at himself too. It was silly, really, how the character of Damien was taken more seriously in this world than the calm, practical man behind the desk. I could feel the conversation warming up and was aware that my next question would probably freeze everything up again. Nevertheless…

'Mike, I'm sorry to have to ask this but were you ever—'

'Yes. Next question.'

'Are you sure you know—?'

'You were going to embarrass us both by asking if I slept with her. Yes, I did. I'm not proud of blurring the line between teacher and pupil but we were consenting adults.'

'Wasn't she sixteen when she arrived?'

'Yes, that's right,' he snapped. 'But it was closer to 2010 when our, er, relationship began.'

'And your wife?'

His mouth formed a thin, tight line. 'She understands that sometimes, in order to create beautiful dances, we must make love.' It was hard to tell if this was Mike or Damien speaking. It sounded equally pretentious and bullshitty either way.

'I see.'

'No you don't. You're not a very good liar, Cherry.'

'No, you're right, I don't. I don't see why you can't teach an attractive, very young woman, far away from home, how to dance without having sex with her.'

He stood up abruptly. I automatically backed away in my chair. He smiled and put out his hand. 'Come here.'

Confused, I replied, 'What are you doing? It's fine if you don't want to answer any more questions.'

He held his hand out still. 'I'm not going to hurt you. I'm going to prove a point. Come on.'

I took it reluctantly and he whisked me out of my chair, through the office door onto the dance floor. My boots clattered noisily and I stood there awkwardly while he walked around me.

'Take those off.' He pointed to my boots. 'And that cardigan.'

'Is this really necessary…' I started to protest.

'Do it. I want you to understand. This will help you work on the show. I don't want to see your wrinkly disapproving look when we talk about the relationship between dance and sex.'

I struggled with my buttons and was almost there. 'It's all everyone has talked about since I started work on this. You're all sex mad.'

He threw open a cupboard in the corner which housed the sound system. 'All I Ask of You' from *The Phantom of the Opera* echoed round the room. He walked back and took me in his arms. He tilted my head away from him. I was only wearing a vest top under the cardigan so the feel of his bare arms on mine was strange. I could feel his breath on my neck and his hard pecs pressed against my boobs. His lips brushed my ear when he said, 'Just listen to the music and follow me.' Goosebumps shot up my arms and my legs felt all rubbery. Round and round we went with his hard, hot body pressed into mine, his skin against my skin. There was nothing I could do apart from relax into his arms and let the hot and cold tingles traverse my body as one of my favourite songs reached a climax.

The music stopped and he gently let go. He looked at me. 'Right *then*, when we were dancing, there was a moment that it felt like sex, yeah?'

I nodded, still feeling a bit disorientated.

'That's what I'm talking about. Imagine that, now, we were doing that all day, every day. I'm an attractive man, you're an attractive woman. Would we want to have sex? Yes. Would our dancing be enhanced by sex? Probably. Would we have sex? Most likely.'

He was right. Even for those few minutes, I could see how one thing could lead to another. I felt flushed and breathless. 'Yes, OK, you win. I won't tell a lie; I can see how that sort of thing could happen. Easily happen.'

'Good.' He smiled, satisfied, and walked back to the office. I scrambled back into my cardigan and hopped through with one boot in my hand.

'Damien, er, Mike, thank you for that. And for talking to me. I can see you're really busy, so I won't take up any more of your time.' I zipped up my boots and began gathering up my bag and notebook. 'Is there anything else you think I ought to know at this stage?'

He was logging into his computer. He stopped and looked at me. 'You know, this probably hasn't got anything to do with anything but there is one thing that's puzzling me.'

'Yes?'

'I want to know why Nadiya's English has got worse in the last ten years.'

'What do you mean by that?'

'I mean, when she had only just arrived in the country, she had pretty much perfect English but now, having lived here on and off for like fourteen years, she sounds more Russian than ever.'

'That's weird.'

'I know. Just thought it might be worth mentioning. Might be related.'

I stood up and shook his hand. 'Thank you, I really enjoyed talking to you.'

He smiled up at me as he held my hand a fraction too long. 'I think we both know which bit you enjoyed the most. Stay safe, Cherry Hinton.'

I was still tutting and rolling my eyes in the car park. I felt all unnecessarily hot and bothered. And I didn't mind that he'd called me attractive. I was so shallow sometimes.

Chapter Nine

I'd totally run out of time to do anything apart from get back to the shop and meet up with D'arcy as I had promised to go through the stock ordering system with her.

D'arcy had come as a pleasant surprise and it wasn't until she began working for me that I realised how much I needed an assistant in the shop. It had all come about because I'd reluctantly agreed to take a work experience student from the local high school. I wasn't very keen but everyone had pointed out the virtue of shop owners getting more involved in the local community and then the leader of Brentwood Council, Boris O'Kane, had pledged that every shop which took a student could have ten per cent off their rates for those two weeks and that pretty much sealed the deal.

She'd completely contradicted my expectations of the surly gum-snapping teenager I'd anticipated. She had been keen, quick to learn and very knowledgeable about cake. She had managed to wait three hours before asking me anything about being on *The Caravan of Love* and my solving of Kenny Thorpe's murder. I liked her; she was like the little sister I'd always wanted. And far less annoying than Kelsey's actual little sister, Kaleese, who was in the same year at school as her. The price to pay for employing D'arcy (aside from her wages and the apprenticeship scheme she was soon to be undertaking after Christmas) was Kaleese carrying on the family tradition of getting in the way of trade. Sure enough as I waved through the window, there she was, phone in hand, classic cherry Bakewell in the other.

'Alright, Cherry?' she greeted me without looking up.

'She's paid for it. I told her after last time if she didn't want anything stale or one of them vegan flapjacks, she'd have to pay,' said D'arcy quickly.

'Them vegan flapjacks are minging, I ain't eating that, am I?'

I must have looked annoyed because D'arcy leapt to their defence. 'Leese, you can't go round slagging off Cherry's cakes like.'

She snorted. 'Call that a cake, 'slike the bits from the bottom of some poncey farmer's market granola stuck together with tasteless glue.'

I squeezed behind them both and dropped my bag in the small back room. I called through to Kaleese, 'How's the dancing going?'

She shouted back, 'I got through to the final thirty of some new stage show that's opening next Easter, didn't I?'

'That's brilliant news, well done.'

'But then they was like, "We wanna be more diverse."'

D'arcy scowled in sympathy. 'And she ain't diverse, is she?'

'What, like, different types of dancing? You can do ballet and jazz as well as street, can't you?'

I walked back through and Kaleese rolled her eyes at me. 'No, duh! Like ethnic diversity.'

'And she's fuckin' white British, isn't she?'

'Even if I'd been a traveller, I'd've had more of a chance.'

They both looked sullen and I wished I hadn't asked. Kaleese was a very talented dancer but then, so it seemed, were lots of other girls. She was studying dance at Chelmsford College in between going for scores of auditions. It was a hard industry to break into. I imagined Nadiya at the same age as Kaleese, coming on her own from Russia to learn to dance with Damien. She was so young.

D'arcy was trying to suggest ways around the issue. 'Couldn't you just pretend to, you know, be a bit black or Asian?'

I jumped in hastily. 'No. Just no. Do not do that. It's wrong and when you make it as a major dance star, as I'm sure you will, it will come back to haunt you. I am sure, when the right part comes along, you'll get it.'

She nodded. 'Yeah, I know, but it's hard not to get a bit down. And Ryan's said he wants an open relationship on top of all that.'

D'arcy looked at me and shrugged. She'd clearly run out of things to say on the matter. I shrugged back and said, 'Then split up with him.'

'What? Then he'll never want to be with me.'

'He doesn't want to be with you now. Open relationships are a way for one person in the relationship to get with more people.'

'No, he said it was so we didn't feel restricted as we were so young.'

'Do you feel restricted?'

'No but...'

'Well, then.' I was feeling cross now. Alright, Kaleese was a cheeky little pain in the bum but she still didn't need some messy-haired, cropped-jean-wearing tosser making her feel like shit. 'There's your answer. Trust me on this one, if he really wanted to be with you, there's no way he'd even contemplate the thought of someone else being intimate with you. Tell him it's over. You want an exclusive relationship or nothing.'

D'arcy joined in. 'Yeah, babe, he's totally not worth it.'

I decided to see how far I could stretch Chris Gordon's gratitude and generosity. 'Look, how about you two come with me tomorrow to see *The Dance is Right* being filmed. I'll introduce you to everyone; maybe you could pick up some tips.'

The girls looked at each other and screamed. Then they grabbed me. 'Cherry, you're the actual best. Wait until I tell Kelsey! Do you reckon she'll lend me an outfit? Aargh, let me update my page now.'

And then she was gone.

D'arcy grinned at me. 'Thank you so much, that's really nice of you. I'm dead excited.'

'You're very welcome. There's not many perks to working for me apart from the stale cakes so you have to take any bonuses I can offer. Now, shall we have a look at the current stock and then we can make a list of what we need?'

'Cool,' she said, 'just going to find a pen.'

And that's when everything went wrong.

The door nearly smashed open on its hinges like in the old days when I'd pissed him off but today it was louder than ever. D'arcy burst through the back door clutching her rape alarm. I turned to her. 'D'arcy, I'm sorry, love, something's come up. Do you want to go have a break?'

She looked from me to Jacob and back again, nodded and walked straight out, flipping the open sign as she did so. Sensible girl.

'I'm only going to ask you once so you'd better not fucking lie to me, Cherry Hinton…'

A cold pain washed over my body. I knew exactly what he was going to ask. Why now?

'Did you have sex with my brother?'

I'm spending the summer selling windows, soffits and facias on the phone to people who haven't asked for me to phone them. It's a crap job but that is surely the point of university summer jobs: to remind you why you are studying for a degree.

I am enjoying a few drinks outside Yates wine bar down by the river when I spot him with a group of friends walking by. The drinks have made me more confident than usual so I call out to him, 'Alright, Felix?' He turns and waves and then jogs back to our picnic table.

'Cherry! Hello you.' He gives me a kiss on my upturned cheek. 'You look great!'

I laugh, a bit embarrassed. 'Um, thanks. You OK? Night on the town?'

'Yeah. Yeah – couple of the lads. I'm working now so don't get too many nights out. Got to get up!'

'What do you do?'

'Investment banking. It's not very exciting but, you know, got to start somewhere. You?'

'Oh me, I'm on summer break from uni. Just finished my second year – I'm doing English lit.'

'Right.' And really that's where the conversation would end if it was a normal person's story and not mine. Instead, I invite him to join us and it becomes quickly apparent to my new colleagues that Felix is only interested in one person at the table so slowly they drift off until it's just us. Of course, I've now had six pints of cider and I'm a flirtatious and sexually active woman of the world. So, there's no reason not to enthusiastically kiss him back when he finally makes his move.

We walk back along the river to where he has parked his car and there's no discussion about what's going to happen next; it just feels fun and right as I straddle him in the back seat of his mum's Ford Mondeo. Afterwards we sit in the front and have a smoke; we chat and put the world to rights. There's no weird atmosphere and no need for a replay. We both got what we wanted and I didn't give Jacob a second thought. Everything between me and Jacob completely ended on that last night at the end-of-sixth-form party and I haven't seen him for two years, so why would I?

'Yes.' There was no point hedging around it.

'And you never thought to tell me?' He was actually shaking. I'd never seen anyone so angry.

My heart was pounding and I could hear the blood rushing in my ears. 'No, it was ages ago.'

'*Six* years ago.'

'Possibly. I haven't thought about it.'

'Oh well, that's great, you not only had sex with my brother but you didn't even think about it? You had completely meaningless sex with my brother? How do you think that makes me feel?'

I felt scared. I couldn't see how he could ever climb down from this terrible rage. It was like he was so angry, he couldn't even see me. 'I… I… it's probably a shit thing to find out.'

'You've no idea. You haven't got the first fucking clue how shit it is. Why on earth did you sleep with him six fucking years ago and yet it took me until fucking yesterday to get you to open your fucking legs?'

'Jacob!'

'Don't come over all outraged, Cherry, you're in no position to be giving me any grief. I loved you. I've spent my whole adult life loving you and this is what you do.'

I fought to keep calm. There was no reasoning with him and his fury. 'Jacob, you know that I've had sex with other people…'

He walked right over to the counter and hissed, 'Yes, but not my fucking brother. Of all the men in the whole bloody world that you could have had pointless sex with, you chose Felix.'

'Jacob, I didn't mean for it… it just sort of happened…'

'Did you even give me a second thought? Did you?'

'No, I didn't. It just was just a heat of the moment, casual pissed-up thing when I was home from uni. We didn't plan anything or lie or anything. I'm so sorry.'

'You're not sorry! You're sorry I ever found out.'

I tried to speak but I had nothing.

'Oh yeah, it was Liz who told me.'

'Liz?'

'Yeah, it seems it was so inconsequential to my brother, he told his wife that you were the best shag he's ever had. How do you explain that?'

My head was spinning. How on earth had that come up in a conversation between Felix and Liz and what was it with the Stow family interpreting events in a completely different way from other participants?

I tried to ask, 'How did he…?'

'Oh, you'll love this one, Cherry. Liz got really pissed at their wedding and wasn't up for it when they got back to the bridal suite so he's, you know, trying to get her interested. When he discovers it's not going to happen, he shouts a load of abusive shit at her. One bit that stood out to Liz was when he told her, "Not that you'd be better than Cherry Hinton, anyway – she was the best fuck of my life."'

I put my head in my hands. I couldn't believe that this had happened. Any of it. From Felix's ridiculous claims to Jacob finding out the day after we finally made our relationship status official. I tried to ask another question. 'And how did Liz—?'

'I picked her up this morning from the hotel as she was having lunch with Mum. We're in the car and she says, "Oh, did you have a good night last night?" And I'm like being a bit coy about it and then she gives it, "I hear you're a lucky man; Felix tells me that Cherry Hinton was the best shag of his life."'

I couldn't believe that anyone would be so thoughtless and cruel to tell their new spouse that someone else was a better shag. Let alone that shag. It wasn't even that good. I debated saying this to Jacob and decided against it. I looked at him and realised exactly what he was going to ask me next. I winced in advance and prayed I was wrong. I wasn't.

'Who was better? Is he a better lover than me?'

'No! I want to be with you.'

'Because I can tell you something, Cherry—'

'No, don't, because you won't ever be able to unsay it and it'll be over then.'

'Cherry, it's already over! You lied to me—'

'No, I didn't, I—'

'And nearly every other shag I've had was better than you. Even Kim Bolton.'

'Jacob, please.' The tears clogged my throat.

'Please, what? I've waited so long for you, Cherry, and you've let me down so badly. It is totally over. Don't call me, don't message me, don't try to contact me in any way. I don't want to speak to you. Fuck, I don't even want to look at you. Just fuck right off.'

Then, it was as if a switch had turned his rage off. He just stopped. He left, gave me one final cold, dead-eyed look and closed the door gently behind him.

Chapter Ten

I'd arranged to meet Nic Johnston early the following morning and then, the plan was, Kelsey and the girls would join me after. No one else was there at the studio when I arrived apart from Nic, who was in the same little makeshift office that we'd sat in when we met Belinda and Jason. Nic was wearing a black V-neck and loose black trousers. Her hair was pulled back into a severe, slightly straggly ponytail and she appeared to have no make-up on. She wasn't a natural beauty but she had a lively and interesting face.

I could barely open my eyes as I'd been up most of the night crying. Kelsey had come straight round to my flat after she'd found the shop shut at three in the afternoon. I told her all of it – the awkward kiss in the DT room, the much less awkward sex in the car and the terrible things that the Stow brothers had said.

She'd not been able to offer up any ideas on repairing the mess – not that I had expected her to. I could see no way of making this better. I just needed to focus on the job in hand and try really hard not to think about any of it.

Nic looked at me and obviously clocked my slitty pig-eye thing. 'Are you OK? We can talk another time if you need to, er…' She fiddled awkwardly with her pen.

'No, no, I'm fine, honestly. Just a bit of man trouble, you know?' I attempted a weak smile.

Nic accepted this and relaxed a little bit. 'Yeah, that's why most of the time I don't bother!'

Was there actually someone involved in this show who wasn't trying to have sex with at least two of the other participants? I felt refreshed.

'So, Nic, as I explained, I'm doing some private work, looking out for Nadiya and seeing if I can find out any more about these… accidents.'

'Yes, so I understand. Do you think they are actually all accidents? It's quite strange, isn't it?' She leant forward and looked at me eagerly, which I found quite off-putting.

I nodded and moved in conspiratorially. 'Well, to be frank with you, Nic, no, I don't think anything of the sort, I think someone is trying to kill Nadiya and I want to know who it is and why. Have you got any thoughts on that?'

She sort of leant back at that, like I'd attacked her with my sudden honest opinion. Her eyebrows shot up her forehead momentarily and I instantly felt suspicious.

'I don't… that's to say, I hadn't really thought… I mean, surely not?'

'You just said yourself that you thought the series of accidents were "quite strange"…'

'Yeah, I know that but it was just an off-hand comment, wasn't it?'

'Was it?'

'What's that supposed to mean?' she snapped back at me with growing annoyance.

I decided to ease off since I would probably be spending more time with her in the future. 'It means that you clearly think something strange is going on here – maybe it's just a feeling you have, or something sort of imperceptible. Maybe people forget about you, watching them from the darkness when they talk or plot or argue?'

She nodded quickly, almost relieved. 'Yes, that's it – you're right. I can't remember when it was, perhaps last Tuesday. Everyone else had gone home and I was just sitting in my usual band seat with my little light on, annotating my music and I heard them.'

'Heard who?' This was good stuff; I'd taken a random stab in the dark when Nic had reacted in a slightly odd way to my question and it seems I'd hit gold.

'Belinda and Alexi. She was saying something like, "You've just got to get rid of her, I don't care how you do it but I'm sick of her hanging about" and he said, "Oh don't worry, I've got the perfect solution. This time it's going to work." And then there was some kissing.'

'And who do you think they were talking about?'

Nic's mean, slightly dull eyes looked at me scornfully. 'Nadiya, of course. They were plotting to get rid of her, surely you can see that? You are a detective, aren't you?'

I decided that I didn't like Nic then. I could see why she was always on her own, perched at her lectern in the dark when everyone else was off gossiping or shagging. I almost wished Kelsey was there to deliver one of her cutting put-downs. I comforted myself by concocting witty one-liners while Nic continued pointing out exactly why Alexi and

Belinda were in it together, but of course, me being me, I didn't say anything, I just nodded and murmured assent.

After that, I thanked Nic for her time and left quickly in search of Nadiya. However, as I descended the stairs, I nearly slapped myself into Damien Spiritwind. A little hot and cold shudder started somewhere under my ribs and rippled down to my feet as I thought about our last encounter. He smiled at me and set me back on my feet.

'Cherry, what a nice surprise!'

And he did look genuinely pleased to see me.

'Damien, lovely to see you too. What are you doing here?'

He looked around, grinning. 'Er, I work here. It's my job to tell the dancers what to do. I'm a choreographer!'

I rolled my eyes and laughed. 'I know that. I mean, don't they know what to do just six hours before the show goes live?'

He laughed and said, 'You'd think, right? They do pretty much but since they're representing me, I like to come down and oversee it. Make sure the group number is really tight, sort out any last-minute issues. I like the buzz too.'

He seemed to be hanging around very early considering the group dance wasn't scheduled for another few hours. Maybe Mrs Spiritwind liked a lie-in on a Saturday. Who was I to be questioning one of the country's top choreographers?

He smiled at me and I felt slightly better for the first time in at least twelve hours. 'Are you OK, Cherry? You look sad.'

'Oh no, I'm fine. Just, you know, relationship stuff.'

'Relationship stuff? I see.'

'Yeah, not that there is a relationship, any more. I mean there was one but now there's not so that's why I'm upset.' I cringed inside. I couldn't fathom why I'd decided to overshare this information with a guy I'd met just once.

'Is it properly over or a lover's tiff?'

'Properly over. He found out that I once had sex with his brother. We weren't together or anything then. Six years ago, so, you know, couldn't cope with that and dumped me.'

Damien considered this for a moment. 'I think the only way you could have done anything worse would have been to have slept with his dad. Or his mum. That would be marginally worse.'

'Ah, OK. Had no idea the whole brother thing was such a big deal. I'm an only child.'

He shrugged. 'I think it's properly over. Shagging someone's brother – it's the lowest of the low.'

'Gosh, Damien, I'm so glad I bumped into you. You've really cheered me up. Not.' But at least he'd confirmed what I already knew. The whole thing was hopeless and shitty.

'Want a coffee?'

'I'd love one but I'm meant to be shadowing Nadiya so I'd best go and find her.'

'That's OK, I'll bring it round for you. You need cheering up.'

I smiled at him. He was a kind man despite being a bit brutal and a bit sexy.

I found her in the dressing room surrounded by short twittery women and Belinda Price. Nadiya was being pinned into a golden sheath dress which sparkled as she moved about. Belinda was wearing a sophisticated navy dress which was slashed to the upper thigh on both sides. I could tell, the instant that I opened the door, both women were unhappy.

Nadiya had the good grace to smile at me briefly when I walked in but I realised that this was because she thought she'd found an ally. 'Look, Cherry agrees, don't you? This dress, it make me look fat, yes?'

'No,' I replied, which was obviously both the right thing and the wrong thing to say. She scowled at me and I felt as though I had failed.

Belinda tried to look reasonable, 'Nads, babe, you look stunning in that dress. Not every woman has got the kind of curves that would make a dress like that work, but you totally can.'

'Are you saying I'm fat? Is that what curvy means, eh?'

Belinda looked appalled and tried a sincere smile. 'No way, Nads, you look amazeballs!'

One of the short twittery women tried to join in. 'Nads, that dress is made for you. You're gunna look so wow tonight, honestly, hun.'

But Nadiya was not having it. 'No. I am not wearing this. I can barely move my legs. How am I supposed to dance an American Smooth when my legs, they only move apart by a little bit?'

Another woman walked around her, surveying the issue. 'Nads, love. We're due on for a final rehearsal in about ten minutes. There's no one else who is the same height as you. We simply can't get another dress in time.'

Then I helpfully chimed in, 'Belinda is the same sort of shape, couldn't they swap dresses?'

Everyone fell silent and looked at me like I'd just dropped a Brussel sprout fart. Belinda was the first to protest. 'Oh no, this is specially made for my presenting duties, I simply couldn't…'

'Yes, I like it. My legs could easily stretch out in this dress. And blue is my colour.'

The first woman, who seemed to be in charge, took out her tape measure from her pocket and whipped it around Nadiya's middle; she then did the same to Belinda, who craned her neck to see the figures but the woman, who I later discovered was called June, was a well-practised professional who was too quick for either of them to see. She started pulling the pins out of Nadiya's dress as she spoke. 'Yes, it'll work. They're almost the same size, give or take an inch or two.'

At this both women glared at each other, trying to work out who was giving or taking the inch, I reckoned. Belinda tried to protest again. 'But navy is such a flattering shade and it'll complement Jason's outfit.'

June ignored her completely and started unzipping Nadiya. She gestured for one of the others to start undressing Belinda. I tried to look everywhere apart from at the two women and failed. Nadiya was wearing more substantial underwear than I'd expected: what looked like a sports bra and a thick nude pair of control knickers. Silvery lines snaked up her torso despite the fake tan. I dismissed them as surgery scars because I couldn't understand why Nadiya would have stretch marks without having been pregnant. Belinda, on the other hand, had on what amounted to three triangles of fabric held together with satin ribbon. I was sure it was very expensive but really, in terms of what it was actually doing, she need not have bothered with it.

Once the two women were redressed to June's satisfaction, they headed back down to the dance floor. Belinda went ahead, shuffling along in the spurned dress. She held her shoes in her hand, which meant that the dress dragged on the floor. Although I couldn't see her face, I could feel that she was seething by the set of her shoulders. Nadiya, on the other hand, seemed to glide along with the fabric swishing around her visible thighs. She did look stunning.

'Cherry, you had brilliant idea. See how good we look. I am glad that Chris ordered you.' She squeezed my arm in the way you see models do for a Christmas shoot when they're trying to show a group of female friends in party wear. I smiled back at her, not really sure where I was supposed to put my hands in return.

Waiting in one of the seats next to the floor was Felix. I hoped against the odds that Jacob hadn't said anything to him. I was unlucky.

'Cherry, I'm so so sorry. I can't believe what got into the stupid little bitch. I've sent her back up north, obviously.'

I didn't know what to say. 'Felix... I...'

'Cherry, it's in the past. Just let it go.'

He seemed to be having some difficulty understanding which of the three of us was stuck in the past. He was the one who'd told his wife that she would never eclipse my Mondeo-based sexual performance and his brother was the one who was prepared to break up with me because I'd had sex with another man six years prior to the start of our relationship. I was pretty certain that the Stow brothers were the ones who couldn't just let it go.

'Felix, can't you talk to him, make him see sense? It was so long ago and so... insignificant.'

A voice chimed in from the back row. Kelsey. 'Yeah, Felix, you made this stupid mess, you should be the one to sort it out.'

He rolled his eyes as if bored already. 'Sorry, Kelsey, I missed the bit where this was your business. If you want to blame someone, blame Liz.'

'She didn't know,' I hissed as Chris Gordon glanced over at us. 'Please, Felix.'

Kelsey added with a slight sense of menace, 'Yeah, cos it would be really bad if this got all over Twitter with the current political situation.'

'Yeah, the media all reckon Cherry's a right slag. So that would be well bad for your political image and that.' Thanks, Kaleese.

'Felix, please,' I tried one more time.

He opened his mouth to protest and was interrupted by Chris Gordon and the floor manager.

'Right, we just want to run through the opening sequence with all the couples and Jason and Belinda.'

'Can we have everyone on the dance floor, please?'

There were six couples left in total so people from around the room started standing up and emerging from the darkness. Nadiya had already leapt to her feet and was halfway across the floor, walking towards Belinda. Belinda had her back to us and was gesturing animatedly to Jason – probably moaning about the dress again. In that moment of busyness, the main lights cut out, plunging us all into darkness. Immediately, I sensed that Nadiya was in danger. I pushed past Felix in order to reach her but I was too late as the noise of a single shot rang out and the screaming began.

I heard Chris call out, 'Get the bloody lights back on.'

There were shouts and murmurs. I heard Jason say in a strangled half cry, 'She's dead. Some bastard has killed her. Help me, over here, help.'

I pushed past someone and moved in his general direction. Just then, the lights came back on and I saw him kneeling on the floor, cradling Belinda in his arms as her blood seeped through the golden dress.

Nadiya began to scream – it was an awful sound, like an animal caught in a trap. Felix tried to calm her down but she shook him off and ran to where Jason was holding Belinda. Jason had gone into shock; he was rocking the body in a slow jerky rhythm. Chris stood looking at the horrible tableau with his mouth wide open. Nobody seemed to know what to do.

'Nic, can you call the police, please?' I was surprised how authoritative I sounded.

A couple of the crew had started over to where Jason was. 'If we could keep the area around Belinda clear and not move anything, that would be great. In fact, what would be most helpful would be if everyone just makes their way off the dance floor and grabs a seat.'

Everyone did as they were asked, grateful probably to be told what to do. Nadiya was still making the terrible inhuman sound; I was beginning to think I'd have to slap her. I put my arm around her shoulders and told her to breathe in through her mouth; she did in shuddering gasps. In between this, she looked at me wildly. 'Cherry, she… she…'

I carried on stroking her back and ssshed her. 'I know, it's a horrible, horrible shock. Keep trying to breathe, love.'

'Cherry, she was wearing my dress!'

I was surprised how callous she was; I mean, it was a nice dress but now it would have a couple of holes and a big stain so it was hardly the moment to be worrying about it. I must have somehow conveyed this on my face because she suddenly took a very deep breath and grabbed my arm urgently. 'Cherry, she was wearing my dress – nobody knew about the change. It was your idea. Whoever shot her thought she was me.'

Chapter Eleven

It seemed like the police had treated the incident with all of the urgency of Kaleese revising for her GCSEs as we sat and waited. Initially, I was concerned that Kaleese would be really upset by the whole thing so I went over to where she and Kelsey were sitting.

'Oh my days, Cherry, this is like the most exciting thing ever, thank you so much,' said Kaleese, half hugging me as she was still sitting down. 'D'arcy is going to be gutted that she missed this. And just cos her mum's car had packed in as well.'

I shook my head. 'Kaleese, it's really important that you don't put anything about this on your social media.'

She made a tutting sound and said, 'Why?'

'Because,' replied Kelsey, 'it's a murder and it's well disrespectful and stuff to Belinda's family so pipe down.'

Kaleese pulled a pouty face and rolled her eyes. Teenagers!

'Did either of you see anything?'

Kelsey shook her head. 'No, I won't tell a lie, it was like complete darkness. I well knew something was gonna happen, though. It was too weird.'

'I know,' I said, 'I thought that it would be Nadiya. I guess the shot must have come from behind me and Nadiya because we were both walking up the dance floor towards Belinda.'

Kaleese interjected, 'Yeah, but how did they know who they were shooting if it was dark? They could have shot anyone. They could have shot you.' At which point she burst into tears.

Kelsey looked at me sceptically. 'Must be delayed shock. Come on, babe, I've got a packet of Minstrels in my bag you can suck on.'

Around the dance floor, I could see the various couples, some of whom I'd met and some who I was sure I would be meeting. It was interesting watching their differing responses to what had happened.

Almost dead opposite us were Jodie and Alexi – they both looked awful. Jodie was crying and clutching Alexi's arm. Alexi looked haunted and stared absently at Belinda's body on the floor. A blue satin sheet, which was to be part of someone's routine, had been found and draped over her but you could still see the dark bloodstain through it and her strappy sandals poking out of the bottom.

Felix was sitting on his own. He had a quizzical look. Maybe he was thinking about how this would affect him in the polls; would the media portray him as the brave hero of the hour or was his involvement in a tacky light entertainment show going to cause damage?

The other couples seemed unbothered, like the host of a show they were on got murdered every day. I saw Joe Rose on his phone; a newsreader who I thought was called Mary Crawford was munching on a packet of crisps. There were two actors from other channels who seemed to be good friends; one was Jack Harrison – he was the show's heart-throb and had enormous muscular arms with which he whanged his partner, Lydia Murino, around with alarming speed and gusto. His friend, Andy Grey, was less fortunate in the looks department but made up for it in character. He played the cheeky, chubby best friend in all of the shows I had seen him in and ran the risk of serious type-casting unless he secured a breakthrough role sharpish. Jack and Andy were comparing pictures on their phones and laughing, which I felt was in bad taste. Up on the balcony, I could see Fanny and Gloria leaning over, trying to see what was going on. They'd only just come on as they weren't needed for the opening section. They looked horrified and stood in silence together.

Nic Johnston sat alone on her stool – away from the rest of the band, who had moved around. The rhythm section were gathered around the pianist and the saxes and trumpets had swivelled around to face each other. Nic scowled into the middle distance and folded her arms. Since she had had the only access to any of the lights during the moment they went off, I seized the moment to go and speak to her.

'Hi.'

She said nothing. Barely even looked up at me.

I pressed on. 'Are you OK? It's a horrible shock, isn't it?'

'I suppose so.'

God, was the woman made of stone? 'Do you think whoever it was meant to hit Belinda?'

'No idea. I guess that's for the police to decide.'

I was about to turn and go back to sitting with Kelsey and Kaleese. This was futile. She was uncharmable. But then she said, 'It's all such a pointless waste.'

'What is?'

'This. It doesn't matter which of them was meant to be hit; it's such a pointless waste of a life.'

I nodded. It was a horrid situation.

Just then, Jacob and his team arrived and I thought that I was going to throw up.

Chris Gordon made his way across the floor towards the three of them. I could see him pointing at Belinda and gesticulating towards me. Jacob glanced over towards me and I saw that his eyes were still burning with the same anger he'd displayed yesterday. He glanced away with contempt written all over his face.

I watched as Ben, Audrey and Jacob walked over to Belinda and lifted the sheet. Probably to check she was actually dead. Jacob pulled out his phone and made a hurried call. Then he addressed us.

'Right, everyone. Thank you for your patience. If I could ask you all to just wait a little bit longer. We'll be coming round to take initial details and witness statements and then you can leave. Obviously, some of you will be required again. I'm sure I don't need to tell you that, for the time being, we don't want any details of what appears to be a murder shared more widely than this room.'

There was a general murmur of assent and the three of them began working their way around the room. I was still standing next to Nic when he walked towards us. I was sure he was going to send one of the others to talk to us. What could there possibly be left to say? It turns out there was plenty.

'Cherry.'

'Jacob.'

'Right then. Can you go through with me what happened, Miss Hinton?'

If he'd called me a cock-hungry slut, it would have hurt less. He was so cold, so cool. He looked straight through me.

'Jacob, I—'

'DS Stow, please, if we're going to do names.'

'Jacob, stop this, it's…'

'DS Stow.'

'Jacob.' I could hear my voice getting really anxious and beggy and hated myself for how desperate I sounded, particularly as Nic was standing there right in earshot of everything.

'DS Stow, Miss Hinton. Are we going to stand here all day or are you going to let me try to solve this murder?' He raised his eyebrows and I saw something that looked like a nasty smirk playing around his mouth. A bolt of realisation told me that he was enjoying himself.

That snapped me abruptly out of whiney mode. 'DS Stow, I would be glad to talk you through this morning's events. Would you like a run-through or would you prefer to ask questions?'

He looked a bit surprised at my sudden change in tack and I felt a low-key sense of victory. 'Er, just a run-through beginning at the time you arrived, please.'

'Righty ho. Well, I arrived early – around, oh, eight thirty hours, whereupon I went directly to the on-set office to meet Ms Nic Johnston.' I pointed to her as she was sitting next to me.

Nic nodded at this and said, 'Yep, that's right, DS Stow.'

I went on, 'So, we talked for approximately twenty minutes and then I came out of the office and had a brief conversation with Damien Spiritwind…'

He held up his hand. 'And he is…?'

Nic seized an opportunity to pipe up. 'The world's greatest choreographer, duh!'

Jacob didn't like that at all. He scowled and replied, 'I was asking Miss Hinton. When it is your turn to contribute, I will invite you to do so.' He sounded so like Mr Hodson, my old head of sixth form.

Nic looked suitably ashamed and crossed her arms.

'He's the show's resident choreographer,' I explained. 'We spoke for a few minutes and then I went to find Nadiya.'

'Why?'

'Because Chris Gordon is paying me a lot of money to look after her so I thought I'd better go and find her.'

'Shame he couldn't afford more for you to protect Belinda too, or is that too big an ask for your limited talents?'

Ouch. I couldn't believe he could be so cruel. The little bit of my self-esteem that had remained intact from the horrid day before curled up inside me and shrivelled to stone. Choking back the tears, I opted to ignore his comments and press on with my statement. 'So then I found Nadiya with Belinda and the dressers. They swapped dresses because Nadiya's was too tight or something and I walked out onto the dance floor, had a chat with Kelsey and Kaleese...'

At this Jacob groaned, 'That's all we need, the fucking ugly sisters getting themselves involved.'

'DS Stow, that is an unnecessary and unprofessional comment. If you will permit me to finish my statement then we need spend no more time having this conversation.'

He rolled his eyes at me. 'Do continue.'

'I spent a few minutes talking to Kelsey and Kaleese and then the call came for everyone to come to the dance floor – they were going to run through the opening segment where they're all on the dance floor having a chat with Belinda and Jason. Then all of the lights went out, there was screaming, a single gunshot sound and the lights came back on. When they did, Belinda was lying on the floor with a wound to her back.'

Jacob consulted his notes. 'Nadiya seems very concerned about the dress; I can't get much out of her.'

'Well, she thinks because they swapped dresses that the bullet was meant for her.'

'And what do you think?'

'I think she's probably right.'

Chapter Twelve

Dead Dance Disaster – heartbreak as Belinda Price dies

By Julia Scofield

The world of dance and television is in mourning today as it has been confirmed that Belinda Price, host of The Dance is Right, *was fatally injured during an incident on set yesterday morning. The police are not able to confirm the details but a source claims that Price was shot by an unknown assailant in what might have been a tragic case of mistaken identity.*

Chris Gordon, the show's producer, commented, 'Our thoughts and prayers are with Ms Price's family right now and we are in discussion as to whether or not this series can continue without her. Viewers should rest assured, though, that we are still committed to producing high-quality Saturday night entertainment.'

'I can't believe I missed it. If only Mum's car hadn't needed a stupid MOT, I'd have seen all the action,' D'arcy grumbled as she dipped her chocolate orange cake pops into their final layer of chocolate and swizzled them round to expertly remove any excess drips. 'Was it well dramatic?'

'Yes,' I replied, passing her the cake-pop stand, 'but not in a good way, in a kind of, I can't believe that this is happening in real life kind of way. Like, one minute, she was bitching with Nadiya over which dress they were each going to wear and next minute, she's dead and the dress doesn't matter any more.'

'That's properly shit, mate.'

We worked in silence for a minute. I contemplated how fleeting everything was. Like one minute, you're on top of the world, you're finally seeing the guy you've liked for ages and then a chance remark brings it all crashing down. Obviously, that wasn't in the same league as being shot but it shows how easily things change.

The day plodded on and I went through the motions of selling cakes and chatting to D'arcy and the customers while, in my head, I flitted between sadness and trying to work out my next move. I really needed to talk it over with someone but I didn't feel that my seventeen-year-old apprentice was the right person for the job. Normally, I would have called Kelsey but I knew that she was taking Kaleese to a big audition for a dance school somewhere up north and I didn't want to bother her. There was only one candidate available.

'Mum?'

'Yes, love, you alright?'

'Yeah, I'm OK...'

'What's wrong?'

'Can I come over after work?'

'Course you can. Will you stay for some tea? I'm doing cheese and potato pie with salad and white chocolate soufflé with raspberry coulis. Is that OK?'

'That sounds lush. I'll see you in a bit.'

Since solving the murder of Kenny Thorpe the year before, I'd been able to afford to move back out of my parents' house.

103

This meant that my relationship with my mum had improved massively as we didn't have to see quite so much of one another. Still, arriving at their bungalow and walking through the door felt like coming home and it was all I could do to not start sobbing immediately. Mum knew something was up and she ushered me onto the settee and thrust a cup of tea into my hand.

'Come on then, this isn't just cos of the Belinda Price thing, is it?'

'No, no, it's Jacob.'

'Oh no, love, I thought everything was alright there. I didn't know you were seeing him again.'

I sniffed hard and sipped my tea. 'I wasn't and then I was and we slept together...'

'Really, Cherry, I don't need all of the details.' This from the woman who frequently berated me for not having got together with Jacob.

'But then he found out that I once had sex with Felix.'

'Felix? His brother? The good-looking one with all the money?'

'Yes, but not like *now*, ages ago – when I worked for Zenith in Chelmsford.'

'He never sold windows, did he?'

'No, Mum. I just saw him when I was working there; anyway, that's not the point of the story.' How did this always happen when we had a conversation?

'And *did* you have sex with Felix?'

'Yes!'

'Gosh! You like to put it about a bit, don't you?'

'Mum! It was one man, about six years ago, one time.'

'And Jacob.'

'So that's two men in six years. Hardly makes me Deep Throat Debbie!'

'Cherry Hinton, don't be disgusting.'

I tutted and drank some more tea.

'So what happened with Jacob, then?' she asked, her nosiness clearly overriding the instinct to avoid entertaining the thought of her daughter having sex with anyone ever.

'He went mad at me for sleeping with his brother six years ago and told it me it was over and he never wanted to see me again.'

'Oh dear.' She patted my hand. 'You probably shouldn't have had sex with Felix.'

'Really? You think? I should have foreseen that in six years' time I was going to want a relationship with Jacob and so should have stopped myself having a bit of fun.'

'Well… it's not much fun for you now, is it?'

I couldn't believe how unhelpful she was being. I was on the verge of leaving before I'd had my cheese and potato pie.

'No, Mum, it's not much fun and to top everything off, I was there when Belinda got shot and I feel somehow responsible.'

She frowned and said, 'Well, love, unless you actually shot Belinda, you are in no way responsible for what happened. You couldn't have done anything about that.'

'Yes, but I think they were trying to kill Nadiya and I suggested that they swap dresses.'

'So then Nadiya would be dead instead? Either way, Cherry, you cannot be responsible for the things other people choose to do. You are not a killer and can't stop people who want to do bad things. The best you can do is be a nice person.'

I felt tears welling up. She was so kind sometimes. 'Mum, I don't know what to do.'

'Well, look at it this way; you can't undo what happened with Felix and Jacob. There's nothing you can say or do that's going to make that situation better for now.'

'Can't I—'

'Think about it, what can you say to change what happened? He's angry at what happened and you can't undo what you did.'

She was right, there was nothing I could do to make Jacob less cross.

She went on, 'The only person who can get over what happened is Jacob and that's his decision, not yours. So, what can you do? Well, you can try to find out what happened – who shot Belinda and why? You can offer Nadiya lots of support and make sure no one tries to kill her again and you can stop this crying and feeling sorry for yourself.'

'Mum, I didn't mean—'

She held up her hand and said quite brutally, 'You made a choice to have sex with Felix and now you have to live with that choice.'

Jesus, talk about tough love. But she was right, sort of.

I was getting into my car, balancing a massive lump of leftover cheese and potato pie on a plate and a Tupperware full of rock cakes, when my phone rang. I nearly dropped everything in surprise as my phone hardly ever rang. It took me a second to work out what the noise was. I put the plate on the seat and fished in my bag for it. Finally, I held it to my ear.

'Hello?'

'Cherry 'inton. It's Leon, Leon Solent.'

'Oh, hi, Leon.' My heart began to pound. Why was the most notorious Essex club owner, gangster and all-round dodgy guy ringing me?

'Cherry, love, are yous involved wiv this Belinda Price business?'

He must have known the answer to that before he asked it; he wasn't a man who asked questions that he didn't already have a good idea of the answer to. It was all part of being a menacing gangster, I assumed.

'Yes, I have been working as a... consultant,' I squeaked.

'Well, it seems you and me might be able to help each other out. I have some mutually beneficial information. And you know what I always say, Cherry. You did me a good turn and I won't never forget that.'

I had, when I worked as a journalist for the *Essex Chronicle* – a long time ago – taken out of circulation one of Leon's biggest rivals, Troy 'the Destroyer' Hatton. This put us on good terms but I was always paranoid that one day it would be me who went for 'a walk in Epping Forest' and never came back.

'Oh, that sounds great, Leon, thank you. When can we meet?'

'You free now? Come down the club and I'll see you there. Tell Lisa on the bar that you're there to see a man about a dog. She'll know what that means – stops the randoms coming in and bothering me. It's 'ard being a celebrity in your own town.'

I knew all about the perils of being a celebrity in your own town and he was right, it wasn't very much fun – but at least people were scared of him. Moreover, I was intrigued as I hadn't really much of an idea where to start with the whole thing. Obviously, I'd only been employed to look after Nadiya, not solve Belinda's murder. I needed a good excuse to get involved.

Chapter Thirteen

A pretty woman wearing elf ears and a ginger wig was behind the bar at Vivid:Lobotomy. There were a few office types in small groups downing their skinny-girl drinks and trying to look as though they were enjoying themselves but otherwise, it was a pretty quiet night.

I approached the bar and smiled and the elf came over straight away.

'Hello, love, what can I getcha?'

'Can I have an Archers and lemonade, please? And also I'm here to see a man about a dog.'

Her finely pencilled-in eyebrows shot up her forehead. 'Sure, let me get your drink.'

I clearly wasn't the usual type of person who saw Leon. She made the drink quickly and dropped a bamboo stirrer into it. Then she came out from behind the bar and led me over to the VIP area. She put the drink on the table and then pulled the table out so that I could slide onto the settee behind it.

'He'll be here in a minute. Can I get you anything else while you're waiting?'

I shook my head and, over her shoulder, I saw Leon appear and walk towards us. He was wearing his usual high-end tracksuit. It looked like it might be Dolce & Gabbana. He wasn't a small man and in the time since I'd last seen him, he appeared to have piled on even more weight around his neck and chin so he looked like an old-fashioned gurner surrounded by a bridle comprising pink shiny flesh. He shimmied up behind the barmaid and ran his hand down her bare shoulder. I saw her repress a slight shudder and turn it into a sort of squeal of excitement as she batted him away. I didn't like it any more than she did but, for now, in this environment, that was simply how things were.

I stood up and it was my turn for a full body grope which, again, hating myself and thinking of all the young girls I knew who were going to have to learn to put up with shit like this, I giggled at and allowed to happen.

'Cherry, lookin' lovely tonight. How's tricks?'

'Oh you know, OK, thanks.'

He sat down next to me and his thigh spilled over and pressed tightly against mine. He slid his arm along the back of the settee and settled his belly on top of his wide-open legs. There was hardly any room for me. 'Good, good, anyway. Don't want to take up all of your evening so let's get to the point, shall we?'

'Yes, please. Go ahead. I'm intrigued.' I giggled and looked at him with wide, awe-struck eyes. I took my notebook out of my pocket to show how big and important I thought he was.

He nodded. He liked that. He liked that I was excited by him. 'Now, you know this dancing programme...'

'*The Dance is Right.*'

'Thas it. So, you know that they have a sponsor that provides all of the luggage and shit.'

'Yes.' I consulted my book. 'LS Furnishings.'

'Thas me.'

'What is?'

'LS Furnishings – that's me, well, I mean that's one of my companies. I've been branching out from the clubs and the snooker halls. Tryin' a bit of retail.'

'I see.' I didn't see where this was going.

'So one of my boys, lovely guy, we call him Russian Pete. Cos he's Russian and that, so he's down at the studio dropping off the gear for this weekend's show and he comes back and tells me that he recognises one of the dancers, that one that dances with that Jodie Banks.'

'What, Alexi?'

'Yeah, that's the fella. But, Cherry, you're not asking me the obvious question…'

I obliged his sense of theatre. 'Where does Russian Pete recognise Alexi from?'

'From his time in a Moscow-based gang. Ask me, go on, ask me!'

He really was like a child.

'But, Leon, what did this Moscow-based gang do?'

He laughed. 'They traffic prostitutes to the UK and America!'

Now wasn't really the time to point out to Leon that he had poor choice in employees but needless to say, I was totally shocked. 'No way. That's horrible. And he's sure is he, this Russian Pete, that Alexi Bondarayev was also in this gang…'

Leon interrupted me by laughing even harder, 'No, no, no – a good-looking guy like Alexi, who can dance like that? He's not in a gang. Oh 'ow innocent you are, Cherry 'inton. No, Alexi's the pimp, innee?'

'I don't get it!'

'He's the bait. He worked the clubs and restaurants, bit of chat here, bit of slap and tickle there, bit of "I have a friend who can get you on a cruise ship slash dancing show slash private members' club", bit of a roofie or whatever the latest shit they use in Russia to knock 'em out and wham bam you're a prostitute in foreign country, ma'am!' He banged his flabby fist on the table and my drink jumped towards the edge.

I put out my hand to steady it. 'Oh no. That's awful. That's a horrid story. I can't believe Alexi would be like that. Russian Pete must have got it wrong.'

Leon shook his head. 'I thought you might say that. I know that you're basically a nice person but that's how you get screwed, Cherry. And I don't want that to happen to you. That's why I'm helping you out. I reckon that this might be the reason for all these accidents on set.'

'What – some, like, weird gangland revenge? And surely, then, Alexi would be the target?'

'Well, I wouldn't be too impressed if one of my top boys turned up on a Saturday night dancing show…'

It all seemed too improbable. 'Maybe he's finished working for this Russian gang and wants to do something nice with his life instead of forcing women into a lifetime of abuse and misery.'

Leon threw back his head and laughed until tears ran down his ham-coloured cheeks. 'Finished working for them? Oh, Cherry, no one ever finishes working for a gang, especially one like Ugroza.'

'Ugroza?'

'One of the biggest organised crime syndicates to come out of that area. Dunno what it means, probably not "helping hands", though, eh?' He laughed again and slapped his thigh.

'So, you're telling me this because…?'

'Because I'm losing money, Cherry. I've paid a fuckin' fortune to have my suitcases, towels, bedsheets and kitchen utensils on the show and unless that twat DC Stow sorts it out pronto, no one's gunna see 'em and, consequently, no one is gunna want to buy LS products.'

Of course, it was always about the money.

'Now, Cherry, no disrespect but the Stow's alright at flicking 'is 'air around and that but I want that show back on the screen by next Saturday. And thas where you come in. I'll give you ten grand to make it happen. How's that sound?'

I could definitely have done with money as I wasn't entirely sure where I stood with Chris since Belinda's death. It didn't seem quite right to be claiming money for keeping one woman alive when another had been shot and killed.

'That sounds good, Leon, but what if I can't make it happen? I mean, I obviously won't take the money but there won't be any other, er, repercussions, will there?'

Leon frowned. 'Just what kind of monster do you take me for, Cherry? Do you think I'm going to hurt you or something?'

'No, no, I just didn't want to disappoint you.'

'Yeah, well, who needs five toes on each foot anyway?'

I gasped and looked at him. At which point he burst into more gales of laughter and pulled me into a tight bear hug. 'Look at you, hahahaha, I promise, no "repercussions" as you so elegantly put it. We got a deal?'

He held out his hand and I placed mine in it. It felt like being squeezed by five hot sausages and a clammy steak. He slid me a piece of paper across the table with Russian Pete's number on it and suggested that I started there.

At last, some possible answers but I definitely needed back-up for this one.

Chapter Fourteen

'So tell me again why we're going to see this Russian bloke?' Kelsey was snapping pictures of her snowflake-encrusted nails for her business page. Apparently, this season was all about looking like Elsa and snowflake chic was the way to achieve this.

I moved over into the right lane and put my foot down. We'd agreed to meet Russian Pete on the neutral ground of Lakeside Shopping Centre but with only five weeks until Christmas, the traffic on the M25 getting there was awful. 'Russian Pete reckons that Alexi is some ex-pimp type for this gang called Ugroza and that maybe there's a link between the accidents and Alexi leaving the gang without permission.'

'Right, but why would they be targeting Nadiya, then, and not Alexi?'

She did have a point.

'Unless,' she said suddenly, 'Nadiya was a sex worker. What if she was part of some deal? You said that she was really young when she came over.'

'Yes,' I replied, warming to the idea. 'What if instead of delivering her to the local brothel or wherever, Alexi actually set her up as a dancer?'

'Yeees, maybe he was like in love with her or something and wanted to protect her so he sent her to Spiritwind and sorted her somewhere to live so she could actually be a dancer.'

'But now, someone has seen them on telly and this Ugroza wants their top pimp back and payment for having scammed them out of a sixteen-year-old sex worker.'

Kelsey looked misty-eyed. 'That's so romantic.'

I took my eyes off the road to look at her sideways. 'What, the bit where the pimp from a powerful gang kidnapped a sixteen-year-old and kept her to fulfil his private desires rather than letting everyone have a go on her? Yeah, it's just like *Romeo and Juliet*, Kels.'

She pouted and huffed, 'OK, maybe not so much that bit. More the saving her from the life of prostitution.'

'Unlike the countless other girls he had deceived over the years…' I said as we finally arrived at the car parks.

'Yeah, well… there's no point getting all moral about it now. Let's focus on this Russian Pete guy. He might have got the wrong person and this could all be a big conjunction.'

Much to Kelsey's irritation, I parked in the car park furthest from the entrance, so I didn't have to try to park between two cars. Parking had never been my strong point and I hated the diagonal spaces they'd put in to save space. She was wearing totally inappropriate open-toed boots with a spiky heel and a kilt. To be fair, I had told her to dress up. I thought it couldn't hurt to get Russian Pete feeling 'predisposed' towards helping us, and Kelsey was very useful in that respect. I had drilled into her that he was a former gangster and still worked for Leon so she ought to at least try to rein in her tendency to be rude. She pulled her puffa jacket more tightly around her face and leant on my arm.

'Christ, Cherry, you might as well have left the car at home and we could've walked here, it would've been about the same distance.'

I laughed. 'It's not that bad and it means we'll be able to get out more easily. Come on, I'll treat you to a pumpkin spiced latte when we get there.'

We had arranged to meet Pete in a coffee shop right by the front doors. I had no idea what he looked like but was hoping he'd look enough like my stereotype of a former Russian gang member to be easy to spot in an Essex shopping centre. We queued up and I glanced around at the other customers: an elderly couple were sharing a Bath bun; a guy with a guide dog was sipping his latte carefully while the dog was licking up some crumbs from the floor; two teenage girls had worn their best clubbing gear to come shopping and were slurping on hot chocolates topped with cream and marshmallows. Clearly, Pete had yet to arrive. Kelsey had chosen a prominent seat, right in the middle of the shop, and when I put her coffee down, she turned it round and took its picture from several different angles.

'Has he got your number?' she asked as she changed the filter on her camera.

'No, but I'm sure we'll recognise him.'

'Not all Russians look the same, you know.' She took a cursory glance around the shop as if to prove her point.

'No, they don't,' said a voice behind us. We both spun round in alarm and there was the blind guy with the guide dog.

Before I could speak, Kelsey asked, 'Are you Russian Pete?'

The man reached for the back of the spare chair at the table and his dog sniffed my leg. I was sure I'd read on some patronising Facebook post that you weren't supposed to stroke a guide dog when it was working but I couldn't resist giving it a surreptitious scratch behind the ears.

He replied, 'Yes, that is what I am known as here. And this is Sparkie.' He indicated the dog. 'Sparkie, sit.'

'Well, yeah,' Kelsey went on, 'cos like in Russia, presumably, everyone is Russian so it wouldn't be much of a differentiator, would it? It would be like calling me Essex Kelsey.'

He chuckled a bit at this and I asked him and Sparkie to join us. Once he was settled with a drink, I thought I'd better get on with the job in hand. 'So, Pete. Sorry, is Pete actually your name? It doesn't sound very Russian.'

He smiled. 'It's Pyotr but your countrymen have problems with this. So, it was Russian Pete or Vlad.'

I laughed. 'That sounds about right; we're not the best at foreign languages. So, Pete, I, er, asked if we could meet because Leon reckons you might have some information about, er, a former colleague.'

'Yes, that is correct. It was last Wednesday. I went with the crew to drop off the selection of luggage for the filming and I recognised him, the man that calls himself Alexi Bondareyev.'

I cleared my throat; how was I going to broach this?

Too late.

'So, Pete, I'm Kelsey by the way, just in case you can't tell the difference between us. Not being funny or nothing but, how did you, er, recognise Alexi when, er, you couldn't, er...'

I had to smile; even she couldn't bring herself to say it.

Thankfully, Pete sensed our shameful inability to express what we meant. 'You are asking me how I recognised Alexi when I could not see him, yes?'

'Yes, sorry,' I said. Adding quickly, 'We don't mean to be rude.'

'It is fine. I have not always been blind.' He removed the dark glasses he was wearing and revealed one of the most horrible things I'd ever seen. His entire eye area was a mass of livid red and purple scar tissue with sunken hollows where his eyes would have been. Kelsey's mouth dropped open and we both just stared, aghast.

She said in horrified awe, 'Shit, mate, what happened to you? Was it some kind of accident?'

His mouth twisted into a sort of smile. 'You could say that.'

I didn't feel that this was the whole story but then it's not really something most people want to rake over – the tale of how you went blind. I moved the conversation on after that. 'You were telling us about how you recognised Alexi…?'

'Ah, yes. So, when you lose one sense, your others become kind of heightened and I recognise steps and voices and the way people clear their throats. I was just overseeing the deposit of the luggage, in a manner of speaking, when I hears this *tappety tap tap* and an *ahem*. I knew it was him.'

Kelsey jumped in again. 'Did you speak to him? Did he recognise you?'

He shook his head. 'We did not speak, no, but he saw *me* and he knew me.'

'Er, how do you know that?' I pushed.

'There was a pause in the *tappety tap* and I heard the breathing, sort of hard and shallow and then he moved away very, very quickly in the direction from which he had just come. Who does that? Who walks along with leisure, stops, breathes very hard and fast and then turns around and practically runs back to where they've come from? A very frightened and surprised man.'

'But, Pete, why would Alexi be frightened of you?'

Pete laughed in his croaky way. 'He is not frightened of me. He is frightened of what I represent. I am a reminder of what he left behind.'

I wanted to test out my and Kelsey's theory. 'Pete, do you know why Alexi left Ugroza? Was it Nadiya?'

Pete shrugged. 'No, I do not know. One day he just left. I thought that maybe he had "gone on holiday" as they called it, *byl utilizirovan,* disposed of. But now he is here and alive. Which is a good thing.'

I thought about this. Had we been too quick to judge Alexi? Maybe he had been trying to get away for a long time and the show had enabled him to do that. 'So, would you say that the people in this Ugroza, would they be prepared to kill his girlfriend as some sort of punishment for leaving them?'

'Yes, of course. Without a second of hesitation.'

Kelsey looked up from where she had been trying to slip Sparkie bits of her gingerbread biscuit. 'OK, so if they won't let anyone leave, how did you get away, Pete?'

He did his half-twisted mouth thing again and lifted the glasses; we both instinctively shied away. 'Kelsey, look at this.'

She turned her head towards him, very slowly.

'They did not want me to be of any use to anyone else so they burnt my eyes away with acid.'

'Fuck.'

'Fuck indeed. And what did I do to deserve such a punishment?' He paused. 'I let a witness live.'

'No,' said Kelsey, shocked.

'You'll like the irony of this, I was *look-out* on the job. They murdered a lawyer and his secretary but we did not know this secretary had brought her child, a girl, to work with her. The child had, evidently, gone to the bathroom and returned to find the crew in action. I grabbed her and was about to strangle her, but she was so small and so innocent that I could not do it. I bound her and shoved her in a cupboard. I thought no one would tell but she did, she told the *politsiya* that a man with kind eyes had saved her. Of course, my boss found out and they took my "kind eyes" as a punishment.'

We both just sat there. What was there to say? It was a terrible story and reinforced how scary the people we were dealing with were. It was little wonder Alexi had run away from Pete when he saw him. How was he supposed to know that Pete had not been sent by Ugroza to find him?

Chapter Fifteen

I begged Chris Gordon for Alexi's address, explaining what I could about his possible involvement with trafficking. Needless to say, Chris was not very impressed and, I think, he was a bit scared too. For all his bravado and domineering ways when he was with women, he had faced little in the way of confrontation in his life – I was sure. I wasted no time in getting round to Alexi's flat, which was only in Brentwood so he would be on hand throughout the season. I assumed that he had a more permanent place which he used when the show was not on.

I banged on the door and when there was no answer, I peered through the letter box. It didn't look very homely at all. Possibly, this was just an expression of the fact he was a sad, single man who didn't really know how to make a place look like home but the stale, unused air suggested that he had left. He'd obviously managed it once before and perhaps seeing Pete again had made him fearful for his life. None of this explained why Nadiya had been targeted, though, unless Ugroza were already onto him. And did this mean that Nadiya was still in danger?

Grateful for not seeing Alexi's dead body splayed out in the hallway, a thought which had been lurking at the back of my mind, I straightened up and turned to find myself face to face with Jacob. I'm not sure how long it took me stop screaming but I was going for long enough to call all the neighbours out onto the landing.

Jacob was blushing furiously and trying to shush me in the same way one might comfort a deranged racehorse. He told the neighbours that everything was fine, I'd just had a nasty shock. Finally, when everyone went in, he turned to me. 'What do you think you're playing at?'

'Me? I'm just visiting Alexi.'

'Right, just a social call, yeah?'

'Yes, just to see how he is.'

'You're not shagging him as well now, are you?'

'Well, I'd originally not thought about it but you know, after one of his lovers was shot and killed three days ago, I was like, "Great, now's my chance – there's a vacancy." So, I thought I'd come straight round and see if he wanted to get it on!'

He scowled at me and tutted. 'Hahaha, very funny. Do you know where he is now?'

'No, I don't, but in the interest of sharing information that might protect him, I've been told that he might have some connection to a trafficking syndicate from Russia called Ugroza and that they might be after him.'

'And you know this, how?'

'An informant.' I wasn't going to share everything I knew with him; I wanted Leon's money. And he had dumped me!

'And you got that information from that informant, how?'

'Blow jobs! Always the quickest way.'

'Get fucked, Cherry. Oh no, you already did *by my brother*.' His mouth twisted into a cruel sneer.

I turned to go; I didn't have to listen to that, especially when I was urgently trying to find Alexi before the Russian mafia did. Like my mum said, Jacob had to sort himself out. There wasn't anything I could do.

'Cherry, come back.'

I turned back towards him. 'What?'

'Do you know where he is?'

'No, I don't. And I *would* tell you if I did because I want him to be safe. Goodbye, Jacob.' I started towards the door. This time he grabbed my shoulder.

'Cherry, wait.'

'Yes?'

It was like that stupid bit at the end of the balcony scene in *Romeo and Juliet* where she keeps calling him back just for the sake of it and he keeps coming back because he loves her. I knew how that one turned out in the end and I wasn't going to keep playing that game.

'Can you contact us immediately if you do see him?'

'Yes. I will. Jacob, you need to know that I do still love you very much but I won't have you keep being rude to me. I know you're really upset and angry and that's OK. I'm going now.'

He opened his mouth to say something but I was already leaving.

I had a pretty good idea where Alexi might be but I didn't want to drive up to Cheshire that evening, so I decided to go and see Nadiya instead. I was hoping she might have a bit more to say about the events of Saturday now that she had gotten over the initial shock of it all. I didn't phone ahead because I didn't want to give her an excuse to be out. I felt that behind all the glamour and perfect toning, there was definitely something she was hiding. It was like she both wanted me to investigate and then found me annoying at the same time. Like someone who wants a French bulldog but then discovers it needs walking and does poos. In light of what Leon and Pete had revealed, it was something to probe further.

Nadiya, like Alexi, lived in a property that had been rented by Expose for the season but it seemed that she was more in favour as she had been given a whole house on Shenfield Green. I'd always been a fan of the Arts and Crafts style properties so I was quite excited to see what the inside of one looked like. As I drove down the High Street, I checked out the fancy bars and the new Italian restaurant that my parents were big fans of. It was funny how when I was growing up, Shenfield had seemed like such a sleepy little place with one café and one Indian and now it was almost a buzzing metropolis. I turned into the crescent-shaped road of the green and counted round to number four. As I pulled into the drive, I saw the curtain at an upstairs window flicker.

I rang the doorbell and waited. And waited. I was just on the verge of having another go when she threw open the door.

'Cherry, it is you. I was not sure who it was and now I must be so careful. Come in.' She waved her hand airily and I followed her. She was wearing what I could gather was standard dancer off-duty wear: brightly patterned leggings and an oversized grey jumper with a high neck that she could cutely nestle her face into when the occasion demanded it. On her feet, she had some high-end sort of slipper shoes that I'd seen advertised in the back of the *Sunday Times*. I guess when you make a living from your feet, you have to look after them with hundred-pound slippers. As I followed her,

I did detect a slight awkwardness of movement and I made a mental note to mention it at the right time.

The house appeared packed with flowers and boxes from posh shops, which were overflowing with tissue paper and items of clothing. On the dining room table was a pile of soft toys. I asked, 'You been doing a bit of shopping?'

She laughed. 'On no, these are gifts from my fans. It is too much. I don't know what to do with it all.'

During my own brief flash of infamy, I'd had the odd bunch of flowers from the petrol station shoved through my letter box and I had thought that that was pretty generous. She swept aside what looked to be several hampers from Fortnum & Mason so that I could sit down. I was sorely tempted to ask if I could have one but it didn't seem like a very classy thing to do. I eyed a tin of fancy shortbread and a bottle of port that were stacked together on the floor. It seemed like a bit of an odd gift to send someone who clearly had to maintain a specific body shape and therefore not eat or drink very much.

She shoved some bears and a box with a pot plant in it off another chair and sat down opposite me. 'Now then, Cherry, why is it that you visit me?'

I decided to cut to the chase. 'How do you know Alexi?'

She frowned, confused. 'I met him through Damien. He was on the circuit, he was good and he needed a partner and Damien suggested me.'

'So, you first met him as a dancer?'

'I do not understand, how else would I have met him?'

I realised I was in danger of doing a Kelsey and accusing her of being a sex worker so I chose my words very carefully. 'I have heard that Alexi was once in a gang and I wondered if you knew about this?'

'A gang?'

'Yes, like a group of criminals.'

'I know what a gang is, I just cannot believe that. When would he have had the time?'

'I think that this was before he met you.'

'No. Alexi is a good man. He is not in a gang. Who is this gang?'

'It's a Russian group called Ugroza.'

Her face visibly paled and she looked shocked.

'You've heard of them?' I probed.

She laughed hollowly. 'Everyone has heard of Ugroza. You hear the stories from your mother about what happens to the kind of girl who goes dancing in clubs. But no, I have no personal association with them. You know what this word, Ugroza, means?'

'No, I don't.'

'It means "menace". Do you think they have something to do with all of these accidents?'

I wasn't sure. I thought back to when I'd first talked to Alexi about it and his words now chilled me: *If it was me, I would not miss; I would cut her throat in the night.* The same outfit who blinded a man for not killing a little girl; would they be so amateurish as to miss three times? Would they not just invade her home while she slept and kill her? It just didn't feel like the work of professional killers.

Nadiya pulled her oversized jumper sleeves down a bit further, thus emphasising the smallness of her hands even more. 'And besides, Alexi, he is not Russian. He is from Ukraine.'

I kicked myself for not remembering this. Sadly, my knowledge of Russian and Ukrainian gang politics was non-existent so I couldn't really comment on whether this was relevant or not. I decided to change tack. 'That's true. I think I'll just have to ask him about it when I next see him. There was something else that I wanted to ask you about, though…'

Nadiya leant forward and did something beguiling with her eyes. 'Yes, of course, what is it?'

'Er, I'm sorry if this is a delicate subject but I wanted to ask about your injury.'

The beguiling look went and was replaced by a wooden mask. 'Yes, what about it?'

'Could you tell me more about that and how it affected your dancing?'

She took a sudden interest in the pot plant that she'd placed on the floor and when she finally spoke, her voice came out flat and monotone. 'I had an accident when I was a lot younger and, for a time, there was no problem with my dancing and then it began to affect my ballroom.'

'What, the actual room?'

'No,' she spat like I was an idiot, 'there are two types of dancing. People who don't know, they call it all "ballroom dancing" but this is two types of dance: Latin dancing and ballroom. So Latin is like, the samba, the cha-cha, the jive, and ballroom is like the waltz and the foxtrot. To be a champion in the Worlds Competition, you need to be able to do all ten. So Latin, that's more sliding your feet forwards and backwards whereas ballroom is much more side to side. And I simply could not do the side to side and the heel leads any more.'

'But on the show…'

She puffed her cheeks dismissively and waved her hand at me. 'The show is not an intense competition. It's like if I was an Olympic runner and for twelve weeks I had to do one fast run on a Saturday, I would be fine because I'm not competing for a medal, I'm not training twelve hours a day. This bores me. It is in the past. Can we talk about the show? You heard from Chris, yes?'

This was clearly a topic that she did not want to dwell on but I needed to ask about her claims against Damien Spiritwind. 'Just one last question, I'm sorry to have to ask this but what happened with Damien Spiritwind?'

She shrugged. 'He taught me to be a better dancer and he taught me to dance like a lover, which I needed to be, to be better.'

I couldn't help but interrupt. 'But you were only sixteen; he took advantage of you.'

She shrugged again. 'Yes, I see that now but, if you want to progress in this world, you sometimes need to let things happen.'

'No you don't! You don't have to have sex with an older man to be a good dancer.'

She looked at me coolly. 'So, Cherry, you are telling me that you've never let a man touch you or look at you when you haven't really wanted to but because it is somehow easier? Because it is better for your career to be a "good girl"?'

I thought back to my last meeting with Leon, to the guys who'd pinched my arse or cuddled me when I was a journalist. To the low-cut tops I'd worn to achieve results with certain interviewees. Did I say 'No, go away you big perv' or was it easier to giggle and put up with it? Perhaps Nadiya was right. Who was I to judge her for not pushing Damien away? Thinking about it, I'd let him paw me all the way around the dance floor without making any kind of fuss at all. I'd even kind of liked it.

I couldn't argue with her without being a liar. She smiled at me, noticing my hesitancy, and said, 'I thought so. It is the way of things. But now I am older, it does not happen so much. Now, you wanted to ask me about the loss of earning suit, I suppose?'

'Well, yes, I mean, if he was like a mentor to you, how did things go so wrong that you needed to sue him?'

The pot plant got the full force of her attention again. I was hoping that I might get offered a drink or a bite of something but it seemed that any level of housekeeping or hosting was a challenge too far for her.

She cleared her throat. 'He should have pulled me out of the ballroom competitions sooner. He kept working and working me; we went to every country to compete and when I wasn't competing, I was on the cruise ships or doing PAs in clubs in London and Paris and New York. My ankle just could not take the pressure. He should have known, but he saw me as a way of making money for him and the dance school. That's why.'

There wasn't much I could say to this. Her complaint sounded reasonable; he claimed to be the expert, but it appeared he'd bled her talent dry. 'I'm so sorry that that happened to you. You must have felt very alone.'

She gave a final dismissive shrug. 'It was OK; I have my family to look after me and Alexi was good to me too.' She got up and said, 'Would you like something to eat? I have been sent these chocolates and I did not want to eat them alone.'

'Oh, yeah, I'm the same once I open the box, that's like, "Oops, the whole lot has gone in one go. How did that happen?"' I laughed and she smiled but not really in agreement – more pity.

She picked up a beautifully wrapped box from one of the low tables that were laden with stuff and peeled off the ribbon and the tissue paper. They weren't like the chocolates that I had at home, which had a legend on the inside of the box to tell you which chocolate was which, but I was sure, by the look of them, that they were all delicious. Rather rudely, I thought, she helped herself first and selected the biggest, fanciest chocolate from the centre of the box. I was left with a more modest one which was a coffee praline by the taste of it. I was happily munching away, planning my next three selections, when she closed the box and put it to one side. I tried to supress my outrage, however; there was a reason Nadiya looked that good and it wasn't from horking down an entire box of chocolates in one go.

My body suddenly felt very weary. It had been a busy few days and, obviously, I'd had the emotional drain of the heartache too. The chair seemed to draw me into it and I noticed that Nadiya, too, was drifting off. It wasn't until she hit the floor and the whole world tilted on a 45-degree axis that I realised something was very wrong. I tried to pull myself out of the chair but it was too soft and it was as if I was attached to it by a magnet. With all my might, I threw my body forwards and landed face first on the cold tiles of the lounge floor. Everything was spinning on a sideways slant. My brain felt heavy and mushy as I fumbled for an answer. Poison. The chocolate. I dragged my phone (which felt like a brick) out of my pocket and pressed the first contact. I didn't even know who it was, I just shouted for help. I was at Nadiya's and I'd been poisoned. My eyelids felt so heavy. I tried to hold them open with my hands but my hands felt like lead sausages. With my last little bit of conscious thought, I stuck my hand in my mouth and poked at the back of my throat. Then that was it.

'Cherry? Cherry? Open your eyes!'

I could hear the voice but it was too far away.

'Cherry! Shit, oh fucking shit. Please, please don't be dead. Can you hear me?'

I could feel warm hands on the back of my head and on my face. It felt nice. Maybe this was death's embrace. I'd expected it to be cooler than that.

'No. No! No! I fucking knew this would happen. You had to get involved, didn't you? And now, now, I'll never be able to tell you that I love you back. And the last thing you said to me was that you loved me. Oh fucking fuck. You died thinking I hated you.'

Jacob.

'Jacob?' I willed my eyes to open and they did by just a slit.

'Cherry?'

'I'm not dead.'

'Thank fuck. Thank you. Thank you. You're not fucking dead.'

'I'm not dead,' I said and burst into tears.

A woman in a green paramedic uniform came into my limited view and spoke to me. 'Cherry, you've been unconscious and I'm afraid you've been sick on yourself. Now we need to get you out of here and into hospital for some testing. We're going to get you onto a stretcher so I just want you to relax. DS Stow, I'm going to have to ask you to let go of her head now and step away.'

'Well, be careful of her head, then.'

'We will, thank you, DS Stow, that's it, move right away.'

I opened my eyes properly now and the ceiling spun like a kaleidoscope. 'I'm going to…' And then I turned and was sick on Jacob's feet. My whole body began to shudder and I could hear beeps and raised voices a long way in the distance. Then it was black again.

The next time I opened my eyes, it was my mum who was anxiously leaning over me. Instead of speaking to me, she threw back the curtain surrounding my bed and started calling, 'Nurse! Nurse! She's awake. Can I have some help here?' I think she thought she was on *Casualty* or something.

'Mum,' I managed to croak.

She dashed over and grasped my hand, which was full of tubes, and I winced in pain. 'Cherry, oh thank goodness. Me and your dad have been so worried about you. How are you feeling?'

'Hungry and sick and thirsty,' I croaked. 'Can I have a drink?'

'Ooh I don't know, love, they've got some sort of drip thingy here to stop you dehydrating. Let's wait until the nurse comes.' She patted my sore hand again.

'Mum, what happened?'

She gave a great big dramatic sigh. 'Well, now, that Jacob Stow will be able to give you more details than me but it looks like you managed to ring Chris Gordon and tell him that you'd been poisoned at Nadiya's so he got straight on to Jacob and they turned up to find you face down in a pile of your own vomit.'

'Urgh, gross. Thanks, Mum.'

'No, they reckon that's what saved you; you had your hand in your mouth like you'd done it yourself.'

I remembered vaguely a spy programme where the hero realised he'd been poisoned and made himself throw up using some salt. Maybe I'd been thinking along those lines.

'I'd hate to think what would've happened if you hadn't… hadn't…' Her chin started to wobble and she let out a huge sob. Thankfully my dad walked in at that point with two coffees and a mince pie. He beamed at me and rubbed my mum's back.

'Come on now, Carol. It's all going to be OK. She's not dead. Pull yourself together, love. I got you a mince pie.'

She sat up and rolled her eyes at him. 'Ugh, you know my opinion of shop-bought pastry, Mike. I don't know why you bother. You might as well just throw your money down the drain.'

'Well, it was all they had. Perhaps you should have packed something if you don't like what's on offer here.'

No one seemed bothered about my brush with death for more than a few minutes. 'Hi, Dad.'

He leant over me and planted a big kiss on my cheek. 'God, you gave us a scare, Cherry. What were you thinking of?'

'Well, I didn't plan to get poisoned, did I?' I suddenly realised, in amongst all of the drama, I'd completely forgotten about Nadiya. 'Mum, Dad, has anyone said anything about Nadiya? She had a bigger chocolate than me and she's not as… um, robust.'

My mum shook her head. 'No, love, I know they brought her here so I'm guessing that she wasn't dead but we've just been here the whole time, haven't we, Mike?'

'How long have I been here?'

My dad consulted his fingers. 'I think this is the third day. Yes, because it was Tuesday and now it's Thursday.'

I tried to sit up, immediately panicked about Alexi. As I did so, I pulled a wire out of something and an alarm went off. Two nurses rushed in and ushered my parents out of the way. They encouraged me to lie back down and reset everything. The curtain opened again and I expected it to be my parents but it was Jacob. A hot flush crawled up my face.

'Cherry, you're OK.'

'Yes, I believe I have you to thank for rescuing me.'

He smiled. 'I think, sadly, you're going to have to thank Chris Gordon first. You did well, though, you pretty much saved yourself. I thought…' His voice cracked and he looked away for a second, trying to get it under control. 'I really thought that you were dead when I got there and I thought that you had died thinking that I hated you.'

I smiled back as best as I could through my cracked lips. 'That would've been a bit shit.'

He sat on the bed and my stomach did a sideways lurch. He picked up the hand without the tubes in it and held my cold fingertips in his hot palm. 'Cherry, I don't hate you. I just…'

'Jacob, it's OK. There's no need for any big dramatics now. Alright? I'm not dead. Nothing else matters now apart from finding out who is trying to kill Nadiya.'

He nodded and put my hand back on the covers. I was pleased with my self-control. I'd been sensible and grown-up about things. Inside, I wanted to throw myself into his arms and beg him to take me back but it was what was on the outside that mattered.

'Jacob, is Nadiya OK?' I realised that he hadn't mentioned her.

'Yes, actually, she seems to have had less of a reaction than you. We can only guess that there was less poison in the chocolate she ate. I mean, don't get me wrong, she was very unwell and they had to pump her stomach and that but she came round properly yesterday.'

'And did you ask her about the chocolates and where they came from?'

He smiled at me again and I felt all nice inside. 'I thought you might like to be there when I did.'

'Yes please.' He looked smug. 'Hang on a minute, where's the catch? What do you want in return?'

'I'd like you to take *me* when you go to see Alexi. Do we have a deal?'

Well, I'd never thought that it was going to happen again – Jacob smiling at me and holding my hand. Wanting to work with me again. It was a shame that I nearly had to die to make it happen but I wasn't going to look a gift horse in the mouth. And so, I agreed.

It took another day for me to get rid of the drip, begin to sip water and generally feel a bit less close to death. All the while, I was acutely aware of the fact that I had failed in the task Leon had set me – finding out who'd done it and getting the show back on air pronto. Kelsey had dropped by with her mobile UV lamp to do my nails but had ended up doing four of the nurses' instead. She was, of course, outraged by what had happened and quick to point out that this was now the fourth attempt on Nadiya's life. This was after she'd had a little cry and declared that I could've been another piece of collateral like poor Belinda.

'The thing I don't get, though, is if you think that it is this, like, dodgy Russian gang, why do they keep mucking up killing her? Aren't they supposed to be good at taking people out? Isn't that, like, what they do?'

I nodded. 'I know, I've thought the same myself. The crimes are all a bit, well, a bit shit.'

'Yeah, I mean, even if they were trying to make it look like an accident, any fool could see now that that many accidents don't happen to one person.'

I sighed. I'd been so excited about the Russian Pete angle but Kelsey had simply confirmed what I'd been thinking.

Someone calling themselves Ugroza wouldn't be going around leaving boxes of chocolate with poison in them in the hope that the woman who hardly ever ate anything might just choose to eat one of them out of the multitude of goodies piled up in her house. It was time to go back to the original list.

'Kels, why does someone try to kill someone else?'

She pondered for a moment and then said, 'Because they hate them and are so overcome with hatred that they lash out.'

'Does this series of accidents seem like that?'

'Well, no – obviously this is planned, innit?'

'OK, so not that then. Why else?'

She rubbed cuticle oil absently into my left hand. 'To get something, money or recognition, like that nutter who killed Kenny.'

'Could this be that?'

'Yeah, but you need to go back to who would benefit from Nadiya's death. Think about it. Who's on the list of people who were there?'

'Felix, Alexi, Belinda, Damien and Nic. OK, so let's take Belinda out for now. Who gets what? Come on, the more outlandish the theory the better.'

She switched to my right hand and frowned and then stopped herself from frowning and jabbed at her brow. 'I need a top-up of Botox; it's been three weeks and I can feel myself having facial expressions again. Right, let's start with Damien – she sued him for loss of earnings and there was an out-of-court settlement. So he hates her and she has never acknowledged the role he had in making her World 10 champion. All he wants is her to say on live telly how grateful she is but she's rejected him and made him a laughing stock.

He burns with well loads of resentment and so he punishes her with a series of accidents to freak her out and make her look like a fool.'

'Yeah, I like that. I can see him being all angry at the injustice of it all. OK, I'll buy that. Who's next?'

'Felix. Did we ever get to the bottom of him shagging her?'

I shrugged and took another tiny sip of water. 'Dunno, everyone seems to be shagging everyone else.'

'Says you!'

'Fuck off, Kelsey. You're supposed to be assisting my recovery.'

'Anyways, let's say he is shagging her – actually, can I just ask and this is relevant, not just me being nosey, but was he, you know, any good?'

'Kelsey! God! I can't believe you asked me that.'

'Yeah, but was he?'

I rolled my eyes and sighed. 'Look, I won't tell a lie. He was certainly the best snog I ever had—'

'Better than Jacob?'

'Only marginally but I liked Jacob more and I was more into it. *So* while the actual kiss was better, the experience with Jacob was actually overall better.'

'Yeah, yeah, but we're drifting away from the point; was Felix a good shag?'

'Kelsey, do we really have to go there?'

She said nothing but raised her eyebrows pointedly.

I sighed. 'I'm seriously not lying here but I was pretty pissed up and I have no definite memory of it. It was OK. Quite nice. Forgettable really.'

'Forgettable?'

'Yup, forgettable.'

She frowned again and had clearly forgotten to preserve her face on any level. 'But didn't he tell Liz that it was the best shag he'd ever had?'

'I know! I couldn't fucking believe it. He must have been winding her up, surely?'

We looked at each other and exploded into giggles. I just couldn't help it.

Then the curtain was whipped back and Jacob walked in carrying a stack of magazines and a tube of Pringles. That shut us both up. He gave me a funny look that I couldn't read and Kelsey saved what could have been an awkward conversation.

'Hi, Jacob. Y'alright, babe?'

'I'm good thanks, just coming to see how Cherry's recovering from her near-death experience. Sounds like you're helping her get over it, though.'

'Yeah, actually you came at a good time. We were just talking about your brother—'

I started frantically mouthing 'no' at her but she wasn't having it and she pressed on, 'We were wondering why he might have wanted to kill Nadiya. Any thoughts on that?'

A vein throbbed on the side of his head and I cringed a bit for Kelsey's sake. He replied, 'Maybe Nadiya knew something about him that could cause him a public disgrace.' He looked straight at me and gave me the same strangely unreadable look. Was he saying I was a public disgrace? I thought we'd moved on from that months ago, but maybe not.

Kelsey just didn't know when to leave things be, though. 'Would Liz leave him if she found out he'd been sleeping with Nadiya?'

Why on earth did we need to keep discussing Felix's sex life? I couldn't think of a subject that Jacob would rather discuss less. I tried to interrupt but my throat was a dry claggy mess and all that happened was a slight croak before Jacob turned to Kelsey and with a murderous look said, 'Why don't you ask him yourself? I couldn't give a shit who he was sleeping with or not sleeping with. But since you're so interested, maybe you could give it a go like everyone else round here.'

He slammed the magazines and the Pringles on the side and yanked the curtain aside and marched out. My eyes began to prickle with tears. 'Kels, do you think he heard us?'

She tutted and rolled her eyes. 'So what if he did? Rude prick. I dunno what you see in him.'

'I know,' I croaked, 'but we'd just started talking again.'

'But, like, literally, what did he hear? You say that shagging his brother was forgettable and that you liked kissing *him* more! It wasn't like you were saying Jacob had a tiny dick and Felix was the ride of your life, was it? Christ, he should've been pleased to overhear that. I tell you, Cherry, he's a self-centred narcissist wanker.'

She was right and I liked her tautological insults. Nevertheless, I didn't want to piss him off before we had the chance to talk to Nadiya about what had happened. My phone pinged with a hastily typed message from Jacob:

Sorry to interrupt. They've dischsrged N but i will tske you to see her on Sat if they let you out.

No kiss. From the man whom I could have sworn was begging me not to die because he loved me. I couldn't believe that he was sending me messages with no kisses. Kelsey was right: even if he had overheard, what right did he have to be cross? I took a deep breath and reminded myself that I had nothing to feel guilty for and it was his problem, not mine. And at least he'd kept his promise. I replied:

Will make sure they let me out. Hope N is not alone.
See you soon xx

'You shouldn't have put kisses if he didn't,' said Kelsey, unsubtly looking over my shoulder. 'You look desperate now.'

'Thanks, mate. I needed to hear that.'

'My pleasure. Now, right, hear me out. Am I right in thinking that Liz Stow is the one bankrolling everything off the back of her handwoven party plates or whatever?'

I forgot about the kisses and refocused. 'Yes, pretty sure that's right.'

'Right, so, he's already been a prick to her – telling her she's a shit shag, being rude about her clothes when we first met her, yeah? So, what's she gunna do when she finds out he's been knobbing Nadiya, eh? So, he needs to silence Nadiya but subtly so he uses a series of "accidents" to do it. What do you reckon?'

I couldn't see Felix going to all that effort when he could just flat out deny that the whole thing ever happened. He was credible and good-looking and Liz was clearly nuts about him to let him carry on the way he had already. But that didn't stop him being a self-serving sleaze so maybe there was another reason to get rid of Nadiya.

I was feeling incredibly tired at this point and my throat was killing me; I think I tried to tell Kelsey this but the next thing I knew, I had come to and it was dark on the ward with just the beeping and swishing of the machines for company.

Chapter Sixteen

I went home to my mum and dad's a day later and enjoyed letting them fuss over me while I lay on the settee watching re-runs of *The Dance is Right*. It was both strange and sad watching Belinda present the show. She looked so glamorous and untouchable, and yet how easily someone had killed her.

My mum came in and sat next to me. 'It's such a shame that she's dead. She was a very pretty young woman.'

I nodded. 'Yeah, I was just thinking that.'

'I mean, she seems so nice; who would have wanted to kill her?'

I looked away from the television. 'Well, that's the thing, Mum – someone's been trying to kill Nadiya. It was an accident.'

She'd picked up the Christmas edition of the *Radio Times* and had her highlighter poised. 'Oh right,' she said, like she didn't believe me.

'What do you mean, "oh right"?'

'I mean that it's funny they've had countless goes at Nadiya and missed and the only one that's actually dead is that Belinda.'

She did have a point. But then that made the whole thing even more stupidly complicated. Was someone trying to kill both Nadiya and Belinda?

My thoughts were interrupted by Jacob ringing on the door. My mum shot up and patted down the back of her hair as she made her way into the hallway. I could hear her twittering inanely as I bent over to put my shoes on. It sounded like she was telling him about her friend Susan's new dog. My mind boggled at the conversational leap that must have taken place from her answering the door and saying hello to saying 'and it jumped up all over my new suede coat, I mean don't get me wrong, it's a lovely dog but you can't get muddy paw prints out of caramel suede'.

I yanked my shoes on and staggered to my feet in a bid to save him but then I heard him reply, 'Well, Carol, if you've got a bit of that carpet cleaner that they sell in Slade's on the Broadway, put that on a damp brush and rub it in, it should sort it.'

I knew that there was a reason he was always able to worm his way back into my affections, despite the scene at the hospital. Eventually, after getting the full rundown on Susan's dog, Maureen's gammy toe and Sandy's sudden death, Jacob stuck his head round the lounge door.

'Alright, Cherry?'

I felt myself go all hot and nervous. 'Hello. I'm ready.'

He came over to the settee and stuck out his hand to help me up. I grasped it and he pulled me smoothly to my feet. He really was very attractive at times.

We walked out to the car with me leaning on his arm like an invalid. My mum watched curiously as he helped me in. Obviously, the last conversation we'd had about all of this was that it was over and he hated me so I knew that I'd be looking forward to the Essex Inquisition when I got home. People say that the Essex Witchfinder General, Matthew Hopkins, was a terrifying man but then they hadn't met Carol Hinton.

Jacob drove a charcoal-coloured Audi A4 which was much more luxurious than my Mini and made me miss my Audi TT that I'd had to give up the lease on when I lost my job on the *Chronicle*. I sank back into the front seat and felt strangely relaxed. My body seemed to be having a full range of responses to Jacob today. He smiled over at me. 'So glad to see you looking a bit better today. I was genuinely scared that you weren't going to make it. Did the hospital tell you any more about what it was?'

'No.' I'd pestered and pestered when I wasn't asleep or out of it but they kept vaguely telling me that their tests had proved inconclusive.

'You were poisoned with cocaine.'

'Cocaine? But I thought that made you, like, euphoric and that, not freezing cold and comatose.'

He turned out of my parents' estate down towards the station. 'The chocolate, according to the early tests pathology ran on what you puked up, was laced with a cocaine serum – it's like a highly concentrated type of cocaine. It would have been deliberately made to, to—' He broke off and coughed.

'To kill whoever ate it?' I finished.

'Yeah.' He swallowed hard and fixed his eyes on the road ahead. Shenfield Broadway was heaving with people stopping randomly and hovering for parking spaces. The rail replacement buses filled the already narrow road and shoppers threw themselves into the street from between parked cars like kamikaze pilots. We turned into Shenfield Green and I was pleased to see that there was a police car with two uniformed officers sitting in it right outside Nadiya's house.

Jacob did an exaggerated whistle. 'Blimey, she's alright for a couple of quid, int she?'

'It's not hers – Chris Gordon has rented it for the season. I think it's part of the deal.'

'Wish my job came with a fancy house.'

'At least you get a car that makes a cool noise and can go through all the lights. All I get is stale cake and poisoned chocolates. Oh yeah, about that, any idea where the chocolates came from? I don't even remember what was on the box.'

'That's probably because there was nothing on the box to remember. We found them and we found the company who sells them but here's the really strange thing: they reckon Nadiya ordered them herself!'

'What? That's mental. I mean, obviously someone has set that up. Why would she order herself chocolates? Wait until we get inside, you'll see, there's absolutely shitloads of food and about the only thing I've ever seen her put in her mouth is protein shake. And that one bloody chocolate, of course.'

We got out of the car and as we walked up the drive to the door, I suddenly felt a bit frightened. I timidly slid my hand through Jacob's arm and he didn't move away.

Nadiya opened the door looking pretty ashen – certainly not the image of health I'd first encountered in the green room on set a couple of weeks before. 'Hello,' she said weakly, 'come in. I thought we'd sit in the kitchen today.' I was secretly relieved. I didn't want to say anything and seem like a big swoony fuss-maker but the thought of going back into that room where it had happened made me feel terrified. I didn't miss the admiring glance Jacob gave her high, rounded bottom as she walked away – which was helpfully enhanced by her skin-hugging leggings. I fought with my face to avoid pulling a nasty scowl.

It goes without saying that the kitchen was all light shades of marble and grey with a massive island in the middle. We slid onto bar stools and Nadiya put the kettle on for tea.

Jacob began, 'So, Nadiya, obviously our liaison officer spoke to you in an official capacity about the events of last Tuesday and you attended an interview at the police station yesterday afternoon. Firstly, I wanted to thank you for your time and reassure you that we will find out who has been committing these crimes and, indeed, who killed Belinda Price. Secondly, I wanted to be clear that I am not here in an official capacity today – I am supporting my friend Cherry, who, as you know, has been privately employed to investigate on your behalf.'

Nadiya smiled at him and looked considerably less unwell. 'Thank you, Jacob. I do feel so… reassured by having you here.'

He smiled back at her – one of his special, extra-sincere smiles that he used to do at the end of his televised crime prevention series, *You're Nicked*. Unfortunately, it got axed as a result of one my investigations, but he didn't seem to hold it against me.

I spoke to bring a halt to the mutual admiration society that had sprung up since our arrival. 'So, Nadiya, I just wanted to ask a bit about the box of chocolates; when it arrived, how it was delivered, etcetera. Is that OK?'

Her face went back to being ill-looking and neutral. 'Sure, go ahead.'

'Right, so, when were the chocolates delivered, then?'

She shrugged. 'I don't know. I have an assistant who comes in on a Monday, Wednesday and Saturday. She usually goes through the deliveries and sorts them out into piles and suggests what we should donate and what we should keep.'

'And have you asked her? What's her name?'

'Lauren. You can ask her yourself.' She pressed something on her phone and a few seconds later, a young blonde woman wearing very tight jeans and a rollneck appeared breathlessly in the doorway.

'Hi,' she said, 'what do you want?'

Nadiya waved a hand at me. 'Cherry Hinton wants to ask you questions about the chocolates.'

Lauren looked at me quizzically and said, ''Ere, weren't you that one on *The Caravan of Love* with that Mark guy?'

Oh great, someone wanting to rake up my shameful past. I sighed; she was only young, I supposed, and didn't know any better. Patiently, I replied, 'Yes, that was me. I was hoping that you might know me better as the investigator responsible for solving the murder of Kenny Thorpe?'

Jacob sniggered next to me. 'I reckon, Cherry, that you could sound a bit more put out if you tried.'

Lauren blushed and stammered, 'Oh my days, sorry, I didn't mean to be rude or nothing.'

'It's fine,' I said. 'Anyways, let's get on with it. Lauren, do you remember a big box of chocolates in a green box with an orange ribbon being delivered?'

'Yes, I do,' she said quickly as if she was trying to please me with her answer. 'I definitely actually remember that, cos we'd just had one delivery from the Parcelforce guy and I thought, *That was strange*, because we don't tend to get any deliveries after him. So yeah, it was a guy.' She seemed to run out of stuff to say then.

I prompted her, 'What was he wearing? Did he come in a car? A van?'

'Oh yeah, that's right. He was wearing a sort of black all-in-one thing and I didn't see a car or van anywhere but sometimes people don't pull actually onto the road cos they think it might be private or something, so they use the layby further up.'

'OK. Did you see his face?'

'Yes, I actually did. He was quite good-looking, a bit swarthy, like.'

I tried a different tactic. 'Is there anyone he reminded you of?'

'Yes, like I was literally thinking, he reminded me of Jack Harrison. Course he was wearing a cap and a scarf round his neck but certainly the bit of his face that I literally saw, it well looked like Jack Harrison.'

I was about to speak when Nadiya interrupted me. 'How the hell do you know Jack Harrison?'

Lauren was taken aback by this and said hesitantly, 'He's on *The Dance is Right* and he plays CJ's brother on *These Days* – you know, that series that's on in the afternoons for old people.'

I nodded. 'It's OK, he's on quite a few things. So, the delivery guy looked like Jack Harrison, yeah? Anything else, like what did he say?'

'Well, actually, he was a bit cheeky. Asked if I got the afternoons off, said this was his last delivery of the day and that he could take me out for a drink.'

Nadiya looked horrified. 'And what did you say?'

Lauren rolled her eyes. 'Well, obviously I said, "Yes, strange delivery driver, I've nothing better to do than go out with random men who knock on the door." What do you think I said?'

Nadiya shrugged and got some mugs out of the cupboard.

I gently asked, 'What *did* you say to him?'

Lauren pouted in Nadiya's direction. 'I actually said, "No thank you, I'm working. That's a kind offer and if you want to DM me I'm on Instagram as LaurenLovestohelp." But I've not heard nothing from him since so I reckon he was just a player trying it on.'

I nodded. 'Yeah, sounds like it. You did the right thing there. OK, so you get the chocolates – how do they arrive? Are they in another box? Wrapped in plastic or anything?'

'No, that's the strange thing. They were like literally just the green cardboard box so I put them in the lounge with the other piles of food. The management of the show tell us that it looks good for us to give food gifts to the foodbank. Especially when we don't eat the food ourselves.' She said this quite pointedly and I was left in no doubt about the relationship that she had with Nadiya and what she thought of her.

Nadiya put down two mugs of very dark brown tea in front of Jacob and I and looked haughtily at Lauren. She said, 'Well, a child could have eaten that and died. And also, the foodbank wants rice, not fancy chocolates.'

Lauren said nothing but turned and walked out. Nadiya opened and closed the kitchen cupboard doors while muttering in Russian.

Jacob and I sipped our tea in the awkward atmosphere and tried to force it down as quickly as possible. He turned on the charm and she thawed a bit. 'Look, Nadiya, we're certainly all pleased that you lived to tell the tale. I can understand that this is a difficult time for everyone. I want you to know that we're here for you.'

She smiled at him and rested her slender, graceful hand on his shoulder. I wanted to flick it off. 'Thank you, Jacob. I feel so safe with you around.'

We got up to leave and then, of the great big long list of people in the world that I would rather not have seen, Felix fucking Stow appeared at the back door. I was shocked so I gobbed out some tea onto the white marble when I realised that it was him. 'Fuck!'

I used my sleeve to try to mop it up. I heard Jacob mutter next to me, 'For fuck's sake, what does he want?'

Only Nadiya seemed in any way welcoming. She at least got up and opened the door for him. He was holding a bunch of flowers from the expensive florist that was just up the road from the house. They used twine and repurposed paper in an attempt to achieve 'sustainability'. Personally, I think any business where you're literally ripping flowers out of the ground to sit in someone's house is going to be problematic on that count but what do I know about such things?

So anyway, he presented Nadiya with a hand-tied lily bouquet wrapped in what looked like a page from the *FT* with a potato print of a star on it. She accepted them like a woman who is used to receiving flowers, i.e. not flapping around trying to work out what surface to put them on, not saying 'Oh really you shouldn't have', and not opening every cupboard in the search for a dusty vase which is either miles too tall or too narrow. She slung them casually on the island and rewarded Felix with a dry-looking kiss. He tried to hold the embrace for a bit longer but she was a seasoned pro who spun out of his grasp both attractively and with minimal fuss. He scowled at both of us and I felt the tension prickle. If only I had drunk my tea quicker, we could have avoided this.

Felix, ever the posh boy wannabe, put out his hand to shake and Jacob reluctantly did. 'Jacob. Good to see you, mate. Cherry.' I got a polite nod and was hugely relieved. I was starting to think that we might even be able to get away without any sort of confrontation but I hadn't reckoned on Nadiya.

'So, Cherry, what is your secret?' She smiled at me icily.

'Sorry, Nadiya, I'm not sure what you mean.' I slid off the stool, picked up my bag and putting it over my shoulder, affecting casualness.

'How is it that you manage to seduce not one handsome man but also his brother?'

Everyone froze like we were taking part in some silly party game. There was nothing to say that could possibly rescue this situation. Nadiya smiled a sort of evil, acidic smile that reminded me of a stereotypical schoolgirl bully. She reminded me of a time I was on a television show called *Mouthy and Menopausal* where the host had tried to accuse me of being a cheater and a flirt. I dug deep into my inner reserves of witty comebacks and replied, 'I dunno, Nadiya. If we're playing Let's Bring Up Indiscretions From the Past, why don't you tell us about how, at only sixteen, you managed to get into Damien Spiritwind's pants?'

Nadiya winced like she'd been slapped. I suddenly felt bad and realised that I'd totally overstepped the mark by blaming a sixteen-year-old who had blatantly been subjected to grooming for being seduced by her much older dance teacher. I was shocked at myself for saying such a horrid thing – no matter how angry I was, it was a nasty thing to say. Way to go, Cherry!

Jacob coughed behind me, but I couldn't quite tell what the sentiment of the cough was. All I knew was that we needed to leave. Then it occurred to me that if Felix had been sleeping with Nadiya, he still ranked me as the best shag of his life. I didn't care if it were true or not; it gave me lots of confidence. 'Nadiya, don't try to rake up the past, please. The most important thing is finding out who has been trying to kill you. I'm surprised that you have any interest in who I've been shagging but, if you've nothing better to do with your time, I suggest you look at the back catalogue of the *Essex Chronicle*, as one of the journalists there has taken a keen interest in my "sexploits". Or, if you're really keen and really don't have a life, you could take Julia Scofield out and ask her all about it.'

Nadiya's neck flared red and her face took on an ugly, twisted sort of look that made Felix step back. 'That does not interest me.'

'Well then, shall we focus on the matter in hand, eh? Jacob and I are going to try to catch up with Alexi. I suggest that you concentrate on getting better and that you don't eat anything that isn't sealed up or cooked by someone you know.'

She didn't even bother replying. She made a small sound like a hmpfh and turned back to the tricky business of drying up the mugs. Felix grinned awkwardly. Momentarily, I entertained the idea that we probably shouldn't be leaving her alone with someone who may, potentially, have been her murderer but frankly, if she was going to talk to me like that, I wasn't all that bothered about looking after her right at that moment.

Chapter Seventeen

I had deduced that Alexi was probably hiding out in Cheshire with Jodie, after seeing how possessive she was. The fact that her house was a long way from the drama and hassle of the show down here in Essex was most likely another contributing factor.

I had swung home after seeing Nadiya to pick up some bits and email D'arcy with some instructions for the next few days. I had a brief flash of guilt but then reassured myself that she was very competent and also most seventeen-year-olds would enjoy the freedom to work and not have the boss around. Mum had readily agreed to go in on Wednesday to cover D'arcy's day at college and had been given strict instructions not to let D'arcy try to use my absence as an excuse for not going to college. She always grumbled because they made her do things like write about marketing and process or practise making complex French pastry fillings when what she really wanted to do was crack on with making exciting new cakes like the one she had planned for the big new opening night of The Crystal Lounge, which had been shut, much to the disappointment of the many Expose tourists, for the last sixth months. It was surprising how easy it was to walk away from everything. Especially when it involved Jacob.

Actually, it was probably better not to question the whole Jacob thing. I didn't know what we were doing. Perhaps now it was evident that I wasn't going to die right away, he was going to go back to wanting me to go away and never come back. I was impressed how he'd managed not to say anything to Felix at Nadiya's but I assumed that he'd had some sort of conversation with him about it before. These were not, however, helpful thoughts so I let him pick up my overnight bag for me and help me into his car. I could really start to get used to being looked after and chauffeured around. It would certainly make my life as investigator loads easier.

We didn't talk for a while but it was a comfortable silence. We'd pretty much made it round the M25 to the junction with the M40 when he said, 'What's the deal with that bandleader? What's she called again?'

'Nic Johnston. I dunno. She's a bit weird – like quite a loner. Doesn't really hang out with the others. Why?'

'I was just thinking about who could have shot Belinda – working through who was there and where they were – in my head.'

I smiled; it was nice to know other people worked the same way that I did. Especially professionals. Speaking of which… 'Er, Jacob, how did you get the time off to come away?'

'It's not time off, though, is it? I told Ben and Audrey to hold the fort and follow up on the ballistics report from the studio and told them I'm looking at the Russian angle. Joys of being in charge these days.'

It was impressive how much better his performance at work had been since he'd stopped performing for the television cameras and just got on with police work. He was right in this case, though: Nic was the big enigma. 'I just don't get what her motive would be, though,' I said. 'She's well into the show, she seems to like Nadiya and the incident she witnessed, she couldn't have actually done it since she was conducting the band at the time.'

He nodded thoughtfully. 'And has she been on the show a long time?'

'Yes, since the start so, like, four years ago. I can't see how there would be any benefit to killing Nadiya. Certainly not in terms of money at any rate.'

'So if it was Nic, it must be for a different reason. Do you think she's attracted to Nadiya?'

It didn't seem very likely or even if it was, that wasn't really a solid motive to attempt to kill someone four times. 'I dunno. If she was, though, wouldn't it be Alexi she'd be trying to get rid of?'

We both sighed. It just didn't feel right.

The rest of the journey passed amicably enough. We chatted about the Russian Pete and Ugroza angle and Jacob received a call with some interesting initial ideas about the gun that had killed Belinda – a small one, apparently.

Jodie's house was on a slightly better than average housing development. Last time I had visited, the whole place had been stripped bare by the bailiffs as Jodie had hit rock bottom both professionally and personally. Today, however, a large red 4x4 stood on the drive and the whole place was adorned with Christmas decorations. We rang the bell and Cindy, Jodie's terrifying slobbery dog, howled the house down announcing our arrival.

Through the door we could hear cries of 'Cindy, no. On your bed! On your bed! Cindy, down! Cindy, no!'

A black shape flung itself at the faux Victorian glass of the front door and claws scrabbled in a mournful attempt to get at us. Then there was a shout in what I assumed was Ukrainian, and silence.

Jodie opened the door and I peered into the hall behind her for evidence that we were about to be mauled to death by the beast of Northwich. Cindy thumped her tail from her tartan cushion in the corner but made no move to attack.

'Hiya, Cherry. You alright? Come in. Ignore Cindy, she's alright – just gets a bit excited.'

We gingerly picked our way past her into Jodie's lounge. It was hugely different from before; she had large settees, a massive telly on the wall, a tree brimming with lights and what looked like a department store display of presents underneath it. She must have seen me looking at it because she continued, 'Bit different to last time, eh? Do you remember, I only had those two garden chairs? Let me go and get some drinks; tea all round?'

Jacob and I said in unison, 'Yes please, white no sugar.'

Jodie raised her eyebrows and said in a singsong voice, 'I'm saying nothing!' as she walked off in the direction of the kitchen.

I remembered that last time I'd come, she hadn't even had any milk and I'd left my rank black tea for Cindy to finish. I was pleased for Jodie because she was a nice woman. What pleased me most, though, was that the walls of the lounge no longer displayed all of the front covers that had been produced during her time in the adult entertainment industry. These had been replaced by a few simple pieces of contemporary artwork and a massive canvas of Jodie with all of her clothes on. It showed how she had moved on from last year, when she was desperate for money and reduced to doing private shows online. Maybe I was just being idealistic but the fact she wanted to display herself with clothes on suggested a newfound self-worth and confidence.

Bizarrely, in amongst this scene of very English decadence and new-made wealth, sat Alexi Bondareyev on a black leather recliner, holding a mug with a half-naked man on the side of it.

'Nice mug, Alexi.' I couldn't help myself.

He nodded and gave a small smile. 'Yes, it is one of these that changes from having clothes on the image to the clothes disappearing when heat is applied. Jodie finds it amusing.'

He said this as if he pitied Jodie getting a bit of fun out of a mug and I found myself disliking him as much as I disliked his former dance partner. My sympathy for both him and Nadiya was waning. I did pause to wonder why, since it was a widely known element of my character to be slightly too sympathetic to people and yet here I was, feeling irritated by him. What right did he have to come to Jodie's house and sneer at her simple pleasures like he was the king of style and good taste? I bit back a retort about his poor choice of clothing also being quite amusing and said instead, 'Really glad to find you here, Alexi. We've been properly worried about you.'

Jacob, who up until this point had been fussing Cindy, unaware of the daggers I'd been shooting, joined in. 'Yeah, mate, would've been useful to leave a forwarding address. We are in the process of investigating a murder here.'

Alexi scowled at Jacob's back. 'Nevertheless, you have found me. I see now why Chris Gordon employed you.'

It was hard with him being Ukrainian to get a full handle on whether this was him being nasty and sarcastic or if I was being overly sensitive.

Jodie bustled back in with a tray that contained three perfectly coloured mugs of tea and a plate of chocolate Hobnobs. Bliss. She put it down on the table and once we were all fully tea-ed and Hobnobbed up, said, 'Right then, in your message, Cherry, you said something about being worried about Alexi. What's the matter?' She reached out and grasped Alexi's hand. He appeared unimpressed by this but smiled at her indulgently as she squeezed it repeatedly like a tennis ball.

'Well,' I began, 'I'm not sure where to begin.'

Jacob smiled at me. 'Just go for it.'

'OK, so, a visitor to the set who is known as Russian Pete believes that he knows you, Alexi, from your association with a Russian crime syndicate called Ugroza.' I stopped, aware that I hadn't actually asked a question but hoping that I'd said enough to get the conversation started.

Alexi shrugged. 'And?' Maybe not.

'And we started wondering if there was any connection between your involvement with this group and the threats to Nadiya's life.'

'Interesting,' he said and leant back.

Jodie had none of his Baltic reserve. 'Oh fucking hell, Lexi, you never told me nothing about no Russians! Jesus Christ, what if they come 'ere and kick off? I don't want no concrete slippers or whatever. Tell 'er that this Russian Paul's got the wrong man.'

Alexi said nothing.

'Tell 'er!' urged Jodie.

Alexi shrugged.

Jacob stopped scratching Cindy's belly. 'I suggest that you consider answering some of Cherry's questions, Mr Bondareyev, or the next time we ask them it will be under caution at Brentwood police station. It's up to you.'

Alexi looked at us all coldly. 'You know nothing of how hard my life has been. You don't know struggle—'

Here we go, I thought, a blow-by-blow account of no Internet, queuing for bread and no Cadbury's Creme Eggs. But Jodie was having none of it. 'Get back in the sea, Lexi! I've spent my whole life battling to stay under ten stone, I've had all my stuff taken away, I had to run a pay-per-view porn hub just to keep a roof over my head and this year I've had a terrible struggle to launch my clothing line and find the right suppliers. You ain't got the monopoly on struggle.'

Alexi's lips quivered with rage. 'Shut the fuck up and let me speak, woman.'

Jodie crossed her arms and glared at him.

He went on, 'You don't know struggle until you have spent a winter without adequate food and heating in Ukraine. So when someone offers you a job – dancing in a club – and says that they will pay for your mother and sister's flat, you make a choice.'

'What sort of job?' I asked.

He laughed. It was an empty, mirthless sound. 'They told me that I was to give the girls a good time. Dance with them, flirt a little. I could "buy" one drink for them from the bar. At first, they tell me that it is so the girls will spend money, will come back and spend money again. And that was all it was at first.'

'So, what happened?' I asked gently, not really wishing to interrupt his flow.

'You have to understand that now they pay for the heating, the electricity, for food parcels that arrive on my mother's doorstep. My sister goes to a good school and has decent clothes to wear. They are both well and happy and warm and all I am doing is dancing and talking and flirting. It feels too easy. And it is. So one night a different guy is in the bar. He tells me that he is wanting to take girls – dancers and au pairs – to UK and USA. He needs someone to tell them about this opportunity and it needs to be someone they like and trust. He says that the pretty ones will do best and that for each high-quality girl who comes over to talk to him about the opportunity once I have set it up, he will give my mother enough to pay the bills for another month. And I do it.'

Jodie is quick to defend him to us. 'See? He didn't even realise he was doing a bad thing. Did you, Lexi?'

He shrugs. 'It is easy now to see where I did the wrong thing but at the time, you want to believe that you are just doing a job. It is clever because it is not me who is benefitting. If it was just my heating and food, when I discovered what was happening, I could walk away. Go hungry, find another job, but not when it is your mother and sister.'

Jacob frowned. 'So when did you find out what was going on?'

'There was one girl, Elena. She was very pretty and we danced many times. She came to the club nearly every night and I had strong feelings for her. I really wanted for her to have this opportunity as I thought she would earn a lot of money as a dancer in the UK. Three days later she is dragged from the harbour – battered unrecognisable. I am not stupid man. So, I think to myself that there have been many girls dying on the road to the airport and at the harbour. I do not put the facts together until one night Elena's mother comes to the club. It is early, the guy is not there and she approaches me. I say that I remember Elena and she tells me that Elena sent her a text from the boat. It is a set-up, there are twenty of them in the hold from all over Ukraine. And that's when I realise. The whole thing and my position within that.'

'So why didn't you just tell them no? That you'd had enough and weren't going to do it any more?' said Jodie indignantly.

I was transfixed by this awful story. I saw Alexi shake his head; how could he put into words this world that was so far removed from ours?

'If I told them no, then my mother and sister would suffer—'

'But they would understand that you didn't want to be part of this criminal gang, wouldn't they?'

He sighed and rubbed his eyes. 'It is not about understanding, it is about the repercussions. They couldn't just let me walk away because I didn't like the way that they made their money. Money that my family used to stay warm and healthy. They would have to punish me, to teach me a lesson first. I was terrified that they might hurt either of them or hurt me so I could not dance; I had to find another way.'

I thought of Russian Pete's face and knew that Alexi was speaking the truth about the cruelty that Ugroza might be prepared to inflict on someone who questioned their methods. Slowly, my view of Alexi was shifting; it seemed he really had been in a position that had left him with only bad choices. I asked, 'So how *did* you get away?'

'The one part of me that wasn't entirely stupid had saved and saved my wages. It seems I was my mother's son as she, too, had saved every little bit of food and money that she could. I think she was wise to what was happening long before me. We agreed that the only way to survive was to tell no one. What people don't know, they don't tell. I sent my sister to school in England; a lot of families do this so it was natural. I changed her name and got a guardian for the holidays. She hated it but she was safe. My mother had an old friend in Switzerland – they had not been in contact for many many years; there was nothing connecting them as they had met by chance when he had visited as a trade envoy. She packed a bag, told everyone that she was going on holiday to Germany and paid a guy to smuggle her over the border when she got there. She sent me one postcard, which intimated her safe arrival. Even I do not know the address of her friend.'

The tension was somewhat broken by Cindy splaying her legs to clean her bottom. She made a big slurpy grunty fuss as she did so and I could feel everyone relax a little bit.

'It's like something out of one of them films, Lexi. You were so clever to hide them both. But what about you?'

'Yeah,' I joined in. 'You're not exactly hiding, are you? You're on telly loads.'

He nodded and smiled. 'What do they call it? Hiding in plain sight? I have a new name; I was a skinny little guy with dark hair and dark eyes and now I am big strong guy with blonde hair and blue eyes. Maybe they watch the telly, maybe they think, *Hey is that little Gregor?* but they can't be sure. But now you tell me, ten years later, that they are here? That Russian Pete has seen me?'

I nodded warily. 'I mean, I wouldn't say "seen" but he thought that you were you, yes.'

'Explain?'

'I'm sorry to say that Pete was blinded, by Ugroza. He doesn't work for them but he wondered if the accidents, Nadiya's accidents, could be the work of Ugroza.'

Alexi looked pale and frightened. When he spoke it sounded as though his voice came from a long way away. 'But how could they know? How in the world did they find out?'

Jodie looked over at him and then back to us. 'You know what, I think that's enough. Poor Lexi has answered all of your questions and you've come round here scaring him like that. I don't think there's anything left to say. If you think he's done something wrong then you can arrest him, DS Stow; otherwise, I think you and Cherry ought to be going. Christ, we're tryin' to get all Christmassy here and you come round and really bring the mood down.'

I felt that this was a bit of a harsh assessment of the facts, since he was the one who had admitted a criminal past in which he'd been part of luring young women into a dangerous scam for cash but I guessed that in Jodie's moral code book, being really very sorry wiped out the sins of the past.

Jacob stood up and brushed the dog hair off his jeans. I got up too and thanked them both very much for their time. Jodie showed us to the door.

''Ere, when you next see that Chris Gordon, can you do us a favour and ask him about the fees for the show. I just wanna know if we will get the full fee if the show gets cancelled. Cos my contract only talks about fee reduction if you get voted off.'

'Sure thing, Jodie. You take care, love.' We had a big hug and some kisses, then she shut the door on us.

Chapter Eighteen

Confusingly, Jacob booked us a room each at the hotel and so I spent an uncomfortable night staring at the ceiling wondering what my next move should be. It felt like we had a reached a crappy dead end both in terms of our relationship and the investigation. All of the answers I got were pointing in different directions and none of them seemed to lead any closer to finding out who was trying to kill Nadiya.

In the end, I got out of bed and made a hasty list:

1. Felix Stow – possibly hates Nadiya; she might be blackmailing him because they have had sex. Pretty flimsy.
2. Nic Johnston – very little to be gained, seems to like Nadiya, jeopardising work if she is the murderer.
3. Alexi Bondareyev – Ukrainian trafficker but lots of reasons to keep a low profile, plenty of other opportunities to kill her.
4. Belinda Price – dead so couldn't have poisoned chocs also unlikely to shoot self dead.
5. Damien Spiritwind – hates Nadiya for suing, possibly underage sex.

There was nothing on the list that convinced me that any one of them was guilty and yet there was no one else it could have been. I needed a new angle on this. Then my phone rang.

'Kelsey?'

'Oh thank God you're there. I thought you might have been riding Jacob all night long and wouldn't pick up.'

'Kels, it's the middle of the night, mate.'

'What? You call seven thirty the middle of the night? You must have some seriously good blackout blinds, babe, that's all I can say.'

I looked at the time on the television. She was right. Had I really been raking over this for that long?

'No, no bedroom action for me. I've been awake all night trying to work out this thing with Nadiya. It's crazy. I can't see how or why any of them would want to do it.'

'Do what?'

'What do you mean?'

'I mean, make Nadiya have accidents or kill Belinda?'

It was like my mum had said and I'd dismissed it then but now I wasn't so sure. 'Keep talking at me, Kels. About Belinda. '

'Well, there's only one dead person, Belinda, so maybe for now you should concentrate on who would want to kill Belinda and how they did it rather than who's trying to harm Nadiya.'

'Yes! Kelsey, you're a genius!'

'Wow! That's not something I hear a lot. Anyways, enough about you, I'm ringing for a reason.'

'Yeah?'

'So Kaleese has got another interview and audition at one of them big boarding schools that's famous for its performing arts and that. Only Mum can't come cos it's the final of the balayage competition on Saturday and she's the regional finalist for north Essex. And it's in the middle of nowhere and you know I can't drive, so me and Kaleese was wondering if you could take us.'

It was a no-brainer. She was my best friend and Kaleese was my surrogate little sister. There was nothing to do but agree. I was rewarded with a little squeal and a threat to drop by the shop as soon as I got back. A wave of tiredness hit me as it sank in that I had literally tossed and turned all night long. I attempted to repair my face – not that there was much point. The feminist in me said that I ought to do my face for me but I would've been lying to myself if I hadn't wanted to look slightly less like a squinty-eyed pug for Jacob's benefit.

He banged on the door half an hour later and shouted that he'd wait for me in the car park. I toyed with bringing up our relationship in the car. I mean, at least he would be trapped for the next four hours but then again, did I really want to push and prod what might be the start of a reconciliation? The decision was taken out of my hands as I slid in when Jacob said, 'I hope you don't mind but I've got a lot to think about on the journey home so I'm just gunna zone out a bit. Maybe you've got a bit of sleep to catch up on?'

Clearly my depuffing hadn't been that successful. 'Sure, I didn't sleep too well last night anyway. Is everything OK?'

'It is. I've got the ballistics report back with a pretty detailed map of where the shooter would have been standing. It's weird but it looks as though they were standing pretty much next to you – almost where Nadiya was standing, if their hypothesis is accurate. Do you remember anyone else on the floor?'

I closed my eyes to try to visualise. Nadiya was just a little bit in front of me, Belinda further away with her back to me, Jason looking back up at the dance floor. I remember the lights going out and – 'Jacob, someone knocked into me in the dark.'

'What sort of knocked into you?'

'What do you mean? How are there different sorts of knocking into someone?'

'I mean, are we talking full body barge? Someone brushing past you? A single flailing limb? Think about it.'

He was right; I guess I'd never really thought about it that hard before. I closed my eyes again and tried to recapture the sensation. 'I'm going to go with a single upper arm and elbow sort of jerking into me – like someone elbowing me out of the way.'

He nodded, considering my answer. 'OK, so we've got someone who has maybe got a pretty good idea where they are going but makes a mistake. Let me ask you something: were you supposed to be there?'

'What, as in, had someone told me to stand on the dance floor at that moment?'

'Yeah, as in could our murderer have known you would be there?'

I thought back again; I saw myself following the two of them out of the dressing room, trotting behind them like an awkward donkey while they were all tall and leggy like thoroughbreds. I think I was trying to reassure them both but, no, there was no reason for me to be on the dance floor apart from the fact I was following Nadiya. I think I could see where he was going with this. 'I was in the way, wasn't I? I was an unexpected obstacle to shooting Belinda. But if someone had wanted to shoot Nadiya, I wasn't – she was to the side and in front of me. Jacob, do you see what this means?'

He took his eyes off the busy M6 and turned to me. 'Yes. Someone was trying to shoot Belinda.'

'Wow.' We were both silent for a few minutes as we both tried to process this.

I was cross with myself. 'I'm such an idiot. I've wasted so much time seeing this as part of the pattern of the accidents and all this time it was something totally separate. I can't believe I didn't think of this sooner.'

Jacob was sympathetic. 'Yeah, but how were you supposed to know that? I think the murderer wants us to think the two are linked so that we did exactly this, focused on reasons to kill Nadiya rather than reasons to kill Belinda.'

'OK, well, when we get back I'm going to find out all I can about Belinda and start looking at it from that way round.'

Jacob shook his head. 'No you're not.'

'What?'

'Cherry, you nearly died at the start of the week. You've been employed to protect Nadiya. Not investigate Belinda's murder. That's my job. You need to go back to work, get well again and crack out some banging cakes. That's what's going to happen.'

'Jacob!'

'No, Cherry. This is not your investigation any more. It's dangerous. You heard Alexi. You saw Russian Pete. I'm not having it.'

'Jacob, is this about us?'

He sighed and rolled his eyes. 'No, it's not. Not everything is about us. In fact, right now, there is no us.'

Ouch. That stung.

He continued, 'I won't tell a lie, I love you and I was terrified that I was going to lose you but I just can't live with

166

the fact you slept with my brother and didn't tell me. I just can't. Sorry.'

I managed to croak out, 'So it's still over?'

'Yeah, it's still over. But I do want to be friends.'

Oh, good. 'OK, well, it's good to be clear about these things.' And then I shut my eyes and pulled my scarf up so he wouldn't see the tears leaking out down my cheeks.

Chapter Nineteen

Since we had only been away for one day, the rest of the week at work dragged. I was tormented by my own stupidity both in not listening to my mum earlier about Belinda *and* for thinking that Jacob and I might get back together. None of this was helped by a visit from Felix.

It was D'arcy's college day, so I was looking after the shop on my own and trying to get ahead with my Chafford Hundreds and Thousands Cupcakes and the Southminceter Pie Cake. D'arcy had also left me a cute little portfolio of designs for The Crystal Lounge cake, which was going to be a massive social media opportunity for us – if we got it right. We'd both been practising our sugar work but neither of us could get the right level of shine on our sugar-glass crystals. I was just carefully painting six prototype crystal pendants with some new iridescent glitter that had come in that morning when Felix stuck his head around the door. I tried hard to look pleased to see him or at least not like I wanted to stab him in the face.

He looked quite pissed off. 'Forgettable, huh?'

Oh shit. What on earth had Kelsey done? 'I don't know what you mean, Felix. Shall we start with "hello" and move on from there?'

'You know full fucking well what I mean. I can see it all over your face.'

Oh shit. So, styling it out wasn't going to be an option. 'I'm sorry.'

'Oh no, Cherry, I'm the one who is sorry. Sorry that my lovemaking is so "nice and forgettable".'

I was actually going to kill Kelsey. And she could forget about going to Kaleese's audition. 'Felix, it's not like that. Look, I don't know what Kelsey has told you about it but…'

'Oh, Cherry, believe me when I say I wish it was *Kelsey* who'd told me…'

'Then who—'

'Jacob!'

'Jacob?'

'Yes, my brother, Jacob. Apparently, he heard you and Kelsey having a right old laugh about it down the hospital. I'm glad that, even though you'd had a brush with death, thinking about my sexual skills could still bring you some amusement.'

Oh shit. So he *had* heard. 'Felix, I'm really sorry. That was a private conversation. I'm sorry that Jacob felt it was worth repeating to you.'

'And is it true?'

Really, what was wrong with the pair of them? They were like children. Couldn't just let it go and exist in the moment. Had to keep going on and on about ancient history. I couldn't believe that the local MP had nothing better to be doing than bitching about some casual sex he'd had years ago. 'Yeah, actually it was true. It was fine. I had a nice time. There's nothing else to say. I'm sorry that I hurt your feelings by talking about it with a friend. To be fair, we were trying to work out if there was a sexual angle between you and Nadiya.'

'Nadiya? Christ no. I'd rather shag Liz!'

I nearly laughed. 'Well, that's good since you're married to the poor woman. Doesn't she ever get sick of how mean you are to her?'

'No, she knows she's on to a good thing. I mean, you have seen her, right?'

'Yes and she seemed like a perfectly nice, attractive woman. I don't know what she's getting out of it, though.'

'This,' he said and grabbed me from across the counter. He pressed his mouth against mine and while I struggled and opened my mouth to protest, he plunged his tongue in and held the hair on the back of my head even more tightly. I scrabbled with my hands against him but could only feel the shards of smashed sugar on the counter. His other hand cut into my upper arm as I twisted and writhed to get away from him. He splayed out his fingers that held my arm and with sickening lurch, I realised that he was trying to caress my breast. I felt for my tiny craft blade that I'd left on the counter and jabbed wildly at his stomach. He gave a squeal like the disgusting pig he was and let go of me. 'You've fucking cut me, you stupid bitch. I thought you liked my kisses.' A small dark red stain bloomed on his shirt.

My breath came out in rasping gasps. 'When I was fifteen and knew no fucking better. Get away from me. Get out of my shop. Get out before I call the papers.'

'You wouldn't dare!'

'Oh really? It's a funny thing about being branded a whore by the media; after the first time you don't give a fuck any more. Try me, Felix, just give me one more excuse.'

'Fuck you!'

'I tell you what, maybe if you were less of a selfish pig in life and in bed, you wouldn't be so fucking forgettable!'

Yes! By the look he gave me in response to this, I'd actually said something to upset him. I was so very angry and disgusted. He gave me one last vengeful look and stormed out.

My hands shook as I tried to clean up the mess but I couldn't seem to get my breath, which is how my mum found me a few minutes later. I really hadn't wanted to tell her because I knew that she would be super angry and would possibly do something that we would both regret but she couldn't let it lie after seeing me in that state.

'It's practically rape. That's what it is. You wait until I report this to the police.'

'Mum, I don't want a fuss. It's probably only sexual assault at any rate. And who are you going to report him to? Jacob?'

She swept the broken sugar off the counter. Her mouth was tight with disapproval. 'There's more than one police officer in the whole county, Cherry. You need to press charges. And to think I voted for him last year. I tell you, if I ever see his smug, smarmy face round here, I'm gonna kick him in the nuts. You wait until I tell your dad.'

'Mum, please don't say anything to Dad. I don't want any more trouble. Please?'

She had rinsed out a cloth and was scrubbing it back and forth across the sticky sugar on the counter. I was worried that she was going to crack the glass.

'Fine. If that's what you want but he'd better not cross my path and I certainly won't be voting for him again. Filthy sleaze pig.'

She finished helping me tidy up and calmed down enough for me to tell her that she had been right all along about Belinda. To her credit, she didn't tell me that she'd told me so but, knowing her, she was saving it up for another occasion. She wasn't going to simply let it slide. She must have gone straight down to Kelsey's salon as no more than ten minutes after my mum left, Kelsey flew into the shop in a similar state of indignation.

'I can't believe it. Actually, I can't believe the pair of them. Jacob carrying on, going running to his brother to repeat what he'd heard. I mean, how fucking petty is that?'

'It is petty. I couldn't believe it. And then he had the audacity to ask me if it was true.'

'What? I mean, what a fucking bell-end. Who even does that? What did you say?'

'I told him it was true!'

'Good. Those brothers are a fucking liability. I can't believe Jacob pied you off again.'

'Yeah.' I stacked up my mince pie cake absently. 'Said he couldn't get over me shagging Felix.'

Kelsey picked up a square from my careful festive arrangement and munched on it. 'This is good. It's like pie and cake. He's a waste-of-time knobber.'

'I know.'

'Well, you would know, you made it.'

'Sorry, I meant, I know he's a knobber. I really do need to move on now.'

Kelsey took a few snaps of my mince pie cake, even going so far as to get off her stool to do so. 'Do you know what would make these cakes even better?'

'I thought you just said they were nice?'

'Yeah, yeah, but if you had, like, a layer of marzipan under the mincemeat, it would be even more lush.'

'Marzipan is a pretty divisive ingredient, though, Kels. This pie cake is about crossing the divide, bringing together the haters at Christmas time. You don't want to be bringing in marzipan at such a crucial time.'

She looked at it thoughtfully and then in true Kelsey style, dropped the subject immediately. 'OK, let's go out on Friday. I've been invited to a VIP event at Hollywoods in Romford so we can get in for free and I'll get some drinks thrown in for making a few positive tweets about it and putting some photos on Instagram. It'll be fun.'

Since being old enough to get into clubs, Kelsey had always been the one convincing me that they would be fun. I hadn't been to a nightclub since we went to Southend last year and I had been papped kissing Mark Byrne. The evening hadn't gone well and Kelsey and I had not spoken for a week so I was a bit hesitant about snapping up this opportunity. Everyone knew that no one ever got with a guy they met in a club unless they were really desperate. Reluctantly, I said, 'OK then but don't forget I've got to drive you and Kaleese to Sheffield in the morning so let's not have a massive one, yeah?'

Chapter Twenty

Hollywoods had completely revamped their VIP lounge and it was actually quite classy. They'd done it in art-deco green, orange and gold instead of the traditional night club colours of black, silver and blue. The PR guy had given us the full lowdown on the new look section and the feelings it was supposed to evoke: 'Hollywood glamour, decadence of a golden age and a Gatsby-esque gaiety'. We'd both raised our eyebrows at this before gratefully accepting a cocktail that was more cheap concentrated orange juice than anything else.

Kelsey had then busied herself taking pictures of everything and then got me to take pictures of her artfully posing against the pillars, the faux cocktail cabinet and peeking out seductively from a handy fern in a bowl. She flicked back through them and changed the filters. 'Jesus, Cherry, you've made me look like Tarzan in the one with the plant. You need to get better at taking my good side. Remember, pictures are always more flattering if you take them from above. I don't even have a double chin in real life but you've given me one. Pretty impressive ugly-making skills, Cherry.'

Bored of being Kelsey's photography assistant, I sloped off to the bar in search of something with a bit more booze in it, whereupon I found hunky soap heart-throb Jack Harrison and his somewhat less attractive friend, the actor Andy Grey, propping up the bar with a selection of cocktails between them.

'How come you got three each and we got a shitty orange juice?' I asked.

'We're more famous than you!' said Jack, laughing.

'Bloody cheek. That's so not true. And my friend is an influencer!'

'Is that right?' said Jack, laughing more. 'I still don't recognise her.'

Andy chipped in, 'Here's the thing, you knew who both of us were whereas we only recognised you so we get more drinks for our combined famousness than you and your friend.'

Jack picked up a blue one. 'Here you go; if you're that desperate, have this one. We've got plenty.'

'No, you're alright. I don't want to be some freeloader anyway.'

'Oh, go on, Cherry, try it.'

So I did and it was nice – better than it looked at any rate. Jack and Andy were good fun to talk to and I thought I'd slip in an opportunity to ask a few questions about Belinda, despite Jacob's warnings. 'So, had either of you ever worked with Belinda before?'

Jack nodded. 'Yeah, so back in the day she used to present this programme called *F**k Buddies*…'

It sounded like another terrible show produced by Chris Gordon. Where did the man get his ideas from? 'Was the concept as bad as the title?'

'Er, yeah, you basically had sex with your friend and then gave them feedback on technique and that while they filmed it.'

'The sex?' I was shocked.

'No, not the sex bit, but they showed you kissing and that. I think my agent was a bit concerned about me getting off with another man so early in my career. Was worried about type-casting.'

'Gosh, that sounds pretty grim. Are you still friends?'

He sighed. 'No, funnily enough, telling another guy that he uses too much tongue and squeezed your balls too hard kills a friendship. But there you go. It is what it is. But yeah, I met Belinda. She'd just made the move across from being a model so was happy to pick up any old shit at that point.'

'And what was she like?'

'I thought she was really nice. Dead professional, didn't moan when certain shots took a long time and we had to keep re-doing bits of dialogue. I think she was one of those women who's way more into men, though.'

'How do you mean?' I looked down and realised that I'd finished the entire blue cocktail. It had certainly had a lot more booze in it than the ones we'd been given.

'I mean, like, she was a bit snarky with the make-up girl and the dresser. Like, you know when someone's eyes go a bit kind of cold and mean and then when they're talking to someone else, they're all sparkly and warm. Like that Nadiya.'

'Nadiya?'

'Yes, she is all sparkles with the guys and cold and mean with the girls. Polite but not very interested in other women.'

I thought that this was quite a perceptive comment from someone I'd previously judged to be a bit of a lad with a serious gym habit. Andy added, 'Belinda was very good at making you feel like you were really important when she was talking to you but the minute you turned away, you could tell you were totally forgotten.'

Jack slid another drink across the bar to me. 'Here you go, try that one. So, why the sudden interest in Belinda – I thought it was some cock-up from trying to kill Nadiya?'

I hesitated; after all, they were there the night she was shot. There was no reason that it couldn't be one of them. 'We think that maybe she was the target in this case.'

'Blimey!' said Jack.

'Belinda, eh?' said Andy. 'Doesn't surprise me that someone would want either one of them dead.'

'Really?' I said. It was the first time I'd heard this sentiment.

'Yeah,' he went on, 'well, neither of them was very nice. They were always bickering about what they were wearing, where the camera was, where the lighting was. It was like a constant battle for who was the "best". 'Cept it was neither of them; they were a pair of bitches.'

This was very interesting. I had spent so long thinking about Nadiya as simply a vulnerable victim that I hadn't really explored the rest of her personality. It had been there all along – in her dealings with Alexi, in the argument about the dress, in the way she had spoken to Lauren and in her attempts to wind me up in front of Jacob and Felix. Perhaps this was why someone wanted to kill her; she wasn't a very nice person.

After my third cocktail, the music seemed louder and more inviting and Jack was even better-looking than I remembered. I needed very little encouragement to join him on the dance floor. The music pounded and the lights flashed, highlighting people around us enjoying themselves. I felt his hand pulling me towards him and found myself straddling his leg while we moved in time to the music. As he leaned in to kiss me, it was like an out-of-body experience. It certainly wasn't me kissing the handsome star of the small screen, Jack Harrison. I hadn't felt so relaxed and happy in a long time. I barely noticed his hands roaming my body as we kissed. I slid my hands up inside his shirt and was met with rock-hard muscle everywhere. I felt a massive surge of desire, so big that I drew back momentarily.

Standing in the VIP area, overlooking the dance floor, was Andy. He reminded me of me as a teenager: always the one on the sidelines watching, never the one doing the snogging or making the gossip. I gave him a wave and he nodded back.

'Are you OK?' shouted Jack in my ear. 'Do you want to get out of here? Come back to mine?'

I dithered. I knew what was on the cards and I felt that Jack was not going to be a complicated twat about it. However, the last time I'd thought I was having uncomplicated sex, it came back to bite me on the arse. I looked back up at the balcony to see if I could see Kelsey but I couldn't. I thought to myself that I would drop her a text later and turned to Jack and said, 'Sure. Let's go.'

It was good, better than good. And Jack was extra obliging in that afterwards he got up, fetched me a glass of water and some towels and announced that he was going to sleep in the spare room since he had a 5 a.m. call for *These Days* and didn't want to disturb me. He kissed me on both cheeks, wished me luck solving the murder and told me to let myself out. The perfect one-night stand.

I came to in the morning after a pretty good sleep, all things considered. I stretched out and inspected Jack's bedroom from my position on the bed. He seemed like a pretty tidy guy: lots of functional white furniture, a few tasteful prints and only one massive picture of himself wearing nothing but a handily placed pineapple that was hung behind the bed. I'm sure I read that pineapples were supposed to be a symbol of welcome and good hospitality. He'd certainly made me feel very welcome. A ginger cat padded into the room and jumped up on the bed to inspect me. After trudging slowly across my hair, it settled down on my chest and began purring loudly. It was a relaxing sensation and I was just drifting off when my eye was caught by something hanging on Jack's mid-century armchair. I wiggled the disgruntled cat off me and slid out of bed.

There, casually draped along the back was a black all-in-one sort of boiler suit. I picked it up and noticed it was made of a stretchy fabric like a cycling outfit or something. It was as Lauren had described it, a 'black all-in-one thing', worn by a guy who looked just like Jack Harrison.

Icy fingers of fear walked their way up my spine and my whole body went cold. What if he was still in the flat? What if the whole point of this 'seduction' was just to get me here alone? I couldn't believe that I had been so stupid as to come here without telling anyone. I also couldn't believe that I'd had so much to drink that I hadn't thought for two seconds that Jack might have had an ulterior motive beyond my red-hot powers of seduction.

Who did I think I was? I was totally still Andy Grey, sitting at the side while my more attractive friends hogged the limelight. I had let my own vanity stand in the way of my safety and this is where I had ended up. I pictured Jacob finding my body sprawled on the bed and discovering that I'd recently had sex with Jack. I imagined his lip curling with disgust, unsurprised by my foolish, impulsive actions as the scene of crime officers took photos of my naked body to look at later.

I remembered that I'd left my phone in the hallway, so I struggled into my dress and pants and cautiously made my way out of the room. I inched along the floorboards towards the front door and nearly vomited with shock when the cat leapt up beside me onto the hall table. Hurriedly, I dialled Kelsey and she answered within one ring.

'Where the fuck are you? Me and Kaleese have been waiting twenny minutes.'

Oh bollocks. I'd completely forgotten about Sheffield. 'Shit, Kelsey, I'll explain later. I'm at Jack Harrison's place.'

'What, like, hot actor Jack Harrison? What are you doing there?'

'Listen, I'll explain later. I have to tell you in case anything bad happens to me. Can you contact Jacob and tell him that Jack has got a suit like the one Lauren described the delivery guy wearing. OK?'

'Jack's got a suit like the one Lauren said the delivery driver had? OK, and when can we, er, expect you?'

I opened my mouth to reply when I heard a big squealing commotion on the other end of the line. I could only make out bits of words: 'It is actually him! How did she… Where did it come from? Do you think her mum…?' Then there was some muffled scuffling and I heard Kelsey say, 'You tell 'er, it won't sound as bad coming from you.' Then the phone was jiggled about and Kaleese's voice came on the line. 'So, Cherry…'

'Yes?' What now?

'I'm really sorry but your picture is on the front of the *Essex Chronicle*.'

'What picture?'

'It looks well like you are snogging Jack Harrison from *These Days* and his hand is halfway up your dress. You look OK in it, though.'

Chapter Twenty-One

Harrison and Hinton Lock Lips

By Julia Scofield

> *The world of television is reeling in shock today after we can exclusively reveal that Cherry Hinton, private investigator and former contestant on* The Caravan of Love *and Jack Harrison, actor on* These Days *and current contestant on* The Dance is Right *were seen leaving a nightclub together. Locked in a passionate embrace, neither seemed to notice anyone else. Hinton has been linked with Mark Byrne, murder victim Kenny Thorpe and, most recently, Jacob Stow, former star of* You're Nicked *and crime-fighting hero. It seems, though, that Hinton hadn't a care in the world as she slipped off with Harrison for what we can assume was a steamy night of passion.*

'It's all just made-up crap about what programmes you've all been on. Was it actually a night of steamy passion, though?' said Kaleese as she attempted to show me the report on her phone. I didn't look because I was driving us to her audition.

'Leese, you're too young to be asking me questions like that,' I replied.

Kelsey shouted from the back, 'Was it a night of steamy passion?'

'I think "steamy passion" is maybe a bit of an exaggeration but yeah, there was *some* passion.'

To which Kaleese, who was sitting in the passenger seat, responded, 'Oh my God, he's so fit. I can't believe that he had sex with you.'

Even Kelsey noticed how rude this was. 'Oi, big mouth, think before you speak. Cherry is an attractive lady – that Jack Harrison is a lucky man.'

Kaleese thought about this for a moment and then said, 'Why don't *you* ever get off with anyone famous? In fact, why don't you ever get off with anyone *full stop*?'

I could feel the tension rise in the car and not for the first time did I congratulate myself on having the good fortune to be born an only child.

Kelsey affected a bored, neutral face and said, 'I'm exploring my sexual identity.'

'What, are you, like, identifying as a fucking fridge or something?' muttered Kaleese.

'I won't explain if you're not going to take me seriously.'

I called over my shoulder, 'I'm taking you seriously, babe. What sexual identity are you exploring?'

'I am exploring romantic asexuality.'

Kaleese looked confused. 'Is that where you have both types of genitals?'

I saw Kelsey roll her eyes in the rear-view mirror. 'No, obviously not. I think, living in the same house as me all of your life, you might have noticed me having a big dick swinging about, mightn't you?'

'Well I don't know, Kels, it's hard to keep up with all your identities, innit? Like one minute you're vegan, next minute paleo and now you're asexual. I'm like gunna have to follow you on Instagram, aren't I, if I wanna keep up?'

I tried really hard not to laugh and, instead, concentrated on the road. The A1(M) was a tricky beast at the best of times but particularly bad when you had a hangover and two bickering sisters in the car with you.

Kelsey sighed and said, 'Look, asexuality is about taking a step back from sexual feelings and re-evaluating my sense of self before I become involved with someone else.'

Kaleese scoffed at this. 'Cos no one wants to have sex with you! I bet if that Jack Harrison had come up to you last night and said, "Let's get it on", you wouldn't've said, "Oh no, I'm being asexual tonight"! You'd've jumped on him like your vibrator.'

'Kaleese!' Kelsey leant over in the seat and tried to get at her while Kaleese squealed and pressed herself against the door.

I pulled over into a layby. 'Right, you two. I'm not being funny or anything but I've got a pounding headache and I've had very little sleep. No offence, Kaleese, but this is one of the last things that I want to be doing right now. So, can the pair of you pack it in with the arguing? If you can't think of anything nice to say to one another, just sit and look at your phones until we get there. OK?'

They both murmured some sort of assent and we drove the rest of the way in cold silence.

The Burntwood Academy for Performing Arts occupied an imposing Victorian building in the middle of nowhere. It reminded me of some sort asylum from a Dickens novel where an innocent woman would end up imprisoned until rescued by her long-lost father. Apparently, it also housed

183

the best dance studios and teachers in the North of England, which is why we were there.

As we pulled up into the visitor parking, Kaleese confided in me, 'Cherry, I'm shitting it. Only dead good people even get an interview. Some people have been here since Year Seven.'

'Well then, you must be dead good if they've seen your showreel and invited you up. Remember, they're not expecting you to be, like, the fully finished article. It is a school, where you're supposed to learn stuff.'

Kelsey added from the back seat, 'Just don't fuck it up and fall over or something and don't be trying to be a smart mouth and giving the teachers backchat. Try an' be like one of them ballet girls that's all skinny and says nothing.'

Kaleese replied in a tearful voice, 'I want Cherry to come in with me, not you.' And got out of the car, slamming her door in the process as if to underline how upset she was by Kelsey's comments.

I turned around to Kelsey, who was studying her phone and avoiding eye contact. 'Come on, Kels, don't be like that. This is her big chance. She's worked really hard for this so telling her not to fuck it up is hardly helpful, is it? Anyone would think you were jealous or something.'

Kelsey looked up at me from her phone and I realised that I'd hit home with my final comment.

'You *are* jealous. Why?'

'Why do you think? She's young and really talented and about to start an amazing journey and there's me, painting people's nails for a living on Brentwood High Street. She could be leading a really glamorous lifestyle; she could be in one of them shows in the West End. What could I be doing? Painting more fucking nails!'

'Oh, Kels, that's not true. You're a really successful businesswoman, you've got thousands of followers, you're your own boss. How many people can say that at twenty-eight, eh? I know it feels a bit crap now but you'll be really disappointed if you don't come in with us. Come on?'

She sighed. 'Alright then.'

By the time I had coaxed Kelsey out of the car, Kaleese had already signed herself in and gone to warm up ahead of her audition. An officious-looking woman in a cheap-looking suit greeted us.

'The, er, parents' tour is starting in a couple of minutes. If you'd like to go through to the Fontaine Room, you can help yourself to some refreshments.'

We walked hurriedly towards the room she indicated. I hadn't eaten anything yet that morning and was gagging for some carbs. Our enthusiasm was rewarded with plates piled high with mini pastries. Lots of thin, posh people were standing around talking like they all knew one another. I overheard a snippet of conversation as I went for a second plateful.

'Of course, Jacinta has had offers from everywhere but it's about finding the teachers to match her unique abilities,' brayed one woman with small pearl earrings and a matching necklace.

Another wearing a piecrust-collared shirt which had been turned up, replied, 'That's the wonderful thing about Tilly: she's so coachable, all of her teachers love to work with her.'

A third woman had entered the 'who's got the best daughter' contest and said, 'Maudie's teacher at the Langbourne said that he had nothing left to teach her; imagine being told that at sixteen.'

They all laughed politely but Woman Three had totally won that round.

I stuffed a few more handfuls of croissants in my mouth and sidled back up to Kelsey, who was snapping pictures of everything. The woman in the cheap suit tinkled a small bell, which got everyone's attention. 'Right then, while the girls and boys are auditioning, we thought you might like to see the facilities that they might be using if they are lucky enough to be offered a place today. Please ask any questions as we go along.'

We left the Fontaine Room and made our way down a dark panelled corridor. She went on as if on autopilot, 'This is the original part of the building that was bequeathed to Lord Arlington in 1853. His son established Burntwood as a source of income from the estate. Of course, then it was just a regular school.'

We then swung into a brightly lit and carpeted corridor adorned with black-and-white photographs, which the woman explained were, 'All of our stars – past and present.'

I was surprised how many famous faces I recognised; one struck me in particular. 'Look, Kels, look who it is!'

'Belinda Price. Wow, she was stunning even when she was a schoolgirl.'

The woman saw that we had stopped. 'Oh, yes, that's terribly sad what happened to her. What a horrid thing.'

'Yes,' I replied, 'it must have been a real blow to the school, losing an alumna as lovely as that.'

The woman pursed her lips. 'I won't speak ill of the dead, but her face was the only lovely thing about her. She was a nasty bully and most of us were pleased to see the back of her.' She'd said all this in a hushed confidential tone. Now she raised her voice again. 'Right then, everyone, let's carry on and look at the dormitories.'

Pearl Earrings caught her by the arm. 'I say, are the girls expected to share? Because Jacinta has very specific needs that require her to have a room on her own.'

Cheap Suit had clearly heard it all before and was ready with an answer. 'I'm afraid they do. We are in the business of training our students to work in the industry, and the skills acquired through living and working with others are often those which come most highly valued by producers, casting and directors. If you'll excuse me.' She glanced up the corridor and called, 'Mr and Mrs Takakuda, you've gone the wrong way.' She dashed off to round up the people who'd decided on their own private route around the school.

We waited for her to return and looked at the photos from what seemed to be the end-of-year shows. They were arty black-and-white shots of small groups of students – the type you see in programmes or on people's websites. It all looked very professional. In one, we spotted Belinda again only younger this time – maybe twelve or thirteen. She was dressed in pair of patchwork dungarees as the Scarecrow from *The Wizard of Oz*. She grinned goofily as she leant on a cheerful, angular Tin Man and the most miserable Dorothy I'd ever seen. The poor girl was very clearly wearing a dress intended for someone a few sizes smaller than her. She looked hot and uncomfortable. She had a bush of matted-looking curly hair with an enormous fringe. Beneath this, her mouth was curled into a scowl. Surrounded by girls who were clearly very happy with her bodies, the photo seemed to highlight her complete lack of self-esteem.

''Ere, I'm sure they put her in the picture just to make Belinda look even better. Seems cruel really. Hopefully she's had some help with her hair by now.'

It seemed a bit mean to laugh but she was such a contrast to Belinda in every way, it was almost comical.

Kelsey looked at it again and put her hand over the fringe, just leaving the girl's face. 'Who does that remind you of?'

The scowl was indeed very familiar to me. 'Nadiya Slipchenko. I'll have to tell her that her bushy-haired doppelgänger once came to school here.'

Cheap Suit appeared again at my elbow and looked at what we were looking at. 'Oh yes, *The Wizard of Oz* in 2008. That poor thing there,' she said, pointing at Dorothy, 'another sad story. Such a talented dancer but, one day, she completely disappeared.'

Kelsey looked at her sideways and the woman possibly realised that telling prospective clients about children disappearing from school was unlikely to impress them or make them want to leave their child in your care. She added hurriedly, 'I mean, she packed her things and was collected by a taxi but we never heard from her or her family again. There you go, that's Russians for you!'

Kelsey and I both looked at each other and I said, 'Er, Russians?'

'Oh yes, we welcome children from around the world here.'

'Do you by any chance remember what that girl was called?'

The woman smiled. 'Of course I do, I am the registrar, it is my job to know every child who passes through these halls. Her name was Masha Konstantin.'

We both sighed slightly. It would have been too much of a lead for Nadiya and Belinda to have come here together and someone have a vendetta against them both for some school-based misdemeanour.

We thanked the woman and continued the rest of the tour. We saw the swimming pool, the dorms, which looked a lot like budget hotel rooms (in a good way), and the main performance spaces. A few more pushy parents asked questions that pointed to how special their child was and the level of treatment they expected as a result. The only thing Kelsey asked, which her mum had told her to, was about GCSE re-takes as Kaleese had failed both English and maths in the summer and needed to have another go.

We arrived back in the Fontaine Room, which had been re-stocked with chunky shortbread biscuits and a proper coffee machine. I think the expectation was that we would mingle until the auditions were over but no one seemed interested in making chitchat. Kelsey and I looked more closely at the surreptitious snap she'd taken of the picture containing ugly Nadiya.

Kelsey ventured, 'It could well be her but I don't get how it would work with her timings. She didn't come to England until she was sixteen and then she went straight to Spiritwind, so what would she be doing aged twelve in a photo *here*?'

'You're right, it doesn't make sense. Maybe it's a relative or something like that who knew Belinda.' A thread of an idea or an echo of something someone had said to me floated around my head as I tried to catch it and pin it down. I couldn't do it. I resolved to shelve the issue until later as I was sure that it would come to me. 'What about Tin Man? Could we find out who she is without looking too weird?'

Kelsey grinned. 'Follow me.'

She held out her phone and we sidled up to Cheap Suit, who was listening with a fake interested expression to Maudie-who-couldn't-be-taught-anything-more's mum, presumably telling her about Maudie's prodigious talent.

Cheap Suit looked relieved to be distracted and gave us her full attention.

'Hello ladies, how can I help?'

Kelsey tapped the screen with her nail. 'Yes, you see the girl playing the Tin Man in this picture, me and my friend here are convinced we know her but we just can't place her under all that make-up…'

Cheap Suit frowned and zoomed in a bit on the face in the photo. 'Oh yes, that's er… Natalie… no, no… Nicky… yes, that's it, Nicky Johnson. She was far more into music than dancing though. Is that who you thought it was?'

I nodded quickly and we both thanked her and hurried away.

Kelsey hissed at me, 'Oh my God! Can you believe it?'

I said, 'There's got to be something here. Three women who all went to school together. One dead, one escapes murder several times and one is a strange loner. If the girl with the bad hair is Nadiya – which I do need to check.'

'I well knew it,' replied Kelsey. 'There was definitely something dodgy about her. Are you gunna ring Jacob?'

I knew that I ought to let him know what we had discovered, especially since I'd been very clearly instructed to stay away from the investigation but, at the same time, he didn't pay my wages and it wasn't like I'd actually been investigating anything. The information had just kind of fallen into my hands. 'I will do but I don't think it could hurt to have a little chat with Nic first.'

Kelsey beamed. 'That is such a good idea. This is well exciting. I really think you're gunna crack it before Jacob does. It has so got to be her.'

Chapter Twenty-Two

In my hurry to get to Sheffield and then in light of the new information we had received, I had totally forgotten about Jack and his boiler suit but it seemed Jacob hadn't. By the time I got in from driving all the way back from Sheffield and finally got around to checking my phone, it indicated three missed calls from Jacob and a text instructing me to call. Ominously, there were also two missed calls from my mum. She was bound to have seen the picture of me and Jack so I knew she would have something to say on the matter. I decided that tackling Jacob would probably be the easier call but I was so tired, it was going to have to wait until morning.

Since it was Sunday, we weren't too busy. D'arcy normally manned the shop on her own but I thought it would be a good opportunity to go in and get ahead for the week just in case I couldn't see Nic at a convenient time. I started working on some royal icing, which I knew would take ages in the mixer, and then dialled Jacob. He answered in under three rings.

'Cherry?'

'Hi, Jacob. You alright?'

'Yup.'

Well, there was no way that he couldn't have seen the picture of me and Jack so I guessed he would be a bit pissed off.

'Right, well, I wanted to see if you'd looked into the boiler suit thing.'

'Yeah? Well, I couldn't exactly go round there and knock on the door and ask to see his clothes. Mainly since he's not a suspect.'

'But Lauren said—'

'I don't care what some dimwit assistant said, loads of people have got all-in-one things for triathlons and such.'

He had a point. It was a bit far-fetched. 'Yeah, it could be that, Jack's a pretty fit guy.'

'Well, you'd know all about that, wouldn't you, Cherry?'

Talk about putting my foot in it. I groaned internally. 'Yeah, Jacob, actually, about that—'

He interrupted, 'It's OK, no need explain yourself to me. You're a free agent. I'm the one who broke up with you, remember.'

'I would say it was more of a mutual agreement.' Who was I kidding?

'Cherry, sweetheart, let's not split hairs, eh? The point is, you are free to sleep with whoever you want. If that's the sort of thing you're into, then go for it.' He said this in a really arrogant, patronising voice that made me cringe.

'OK, fine. Whatever. You also need to know that Belinda and Nic Johnston went to school together. And possibly Nadiya or someone who looks like her.'

There was a pause. 'Er, thanks, not entirely sure how that's of any use to anyone, but thank you.'

I felt totally dismissed. What was the point in pursuing this with him? He was clearly in the mood for being a knob.

I was going to have to follow through with my original plan and talk to Nic on my own.

'OK, then. Well, I'll let you get on,' I said in a small voice.

'Yeah, I'm actually really busy today. I'm going out for lunch.'

He clearly wanted me to ask so I obliged him. 'That's nice, who with?'

'Do you remember Kim Bolton?'

Of course I bloody well remembered Kim Bolton. She was a model whom Jacob had briefly dated last year. She had fake boobs, no opinions of her own and an annoying laugh. I couldn't fucking believe it. This had to be linked to the Jack thing, surely? I did my best to style it out.

'Yeah, I remember Kim. How nice to meet up with old friends.'

'Well, I think we might be more than just friends, Cherry, if you know what I mean.'

'What was it you said when you last broke up with her – "it was like dating a really good-looking broom"? Has she grown a personality since then?'

'Cherry, you're starting to sound a little bit jealous. It doesn't suit you, darling.'

My blood boiled. I wanted to reach down the phone and punch his patronising voice out of his throat. 'Well, have a nice time. And don't get any splinters.' I hung up. 'You fucking prick!'

I yanked the bowl of icing out of the KitchenAid where it was still not quite stiff enough and beat it by hand with a whisk. Over and over I dug the whisk in and out until finally it was done. I put the bowl down on the counter and leant back, panting with the effort of it. I hated him. I actually hated him. Well, there was no way that we were going to get back together now. Our whole relationship had clearly been a joke to him anyway since he had found it so easy to slide back into seeing Kim. And the worst thing was, I had to pretend everything was OK because I'd been seen publicly with Jack, which made Jacob look like the injured party.

The whole thing was ridiculous – like a stupid plotline from one of the dreadful reality soaps that Kelsey and Kaleese liked to watch. I always wondered how in real life people constantly split up and got off with other people only to get together again the week after. Only now this was actually my life. Except it wasn't. Not any more. I couldn't undo what happened between me and Felix and Jacob couldn't live with the fact I'd had a single mediocre sexual encounter with his brother despite, as he and Felix claimed, having always loved me, so this was where this storyline finished. I was going to write myself out of the Jacob and Cherry Show and find a breakout career – preferably as a private investigator.

With my mind made up, I rang Nic and left a message demanding to see her urgently, possibly today. I half-heartedly used my royal icing to pipe some trad shells around the bottom tier of the wedding cake I was working on. D'arcy had suggested that we got a stand at the wedding fair at the Brentwood Centre so we were working on a traditional one and a recreation of Michelle and Jon's wedding cake, which had been a model of Colchester Zoo to commemorate their first date. D'arcy had spent hours painting the spots on the giraffes and forming piles of elephant dung out of ganache.

I had finished the first three tiers and Nic had still not replied. I couldn't face talking to my mum yet so I decided to go and see if Nic was home. I had her address from the file that Chris Gordon had given me and it wasn't far. Mindful of how scared I'd been the last time I went somewhere without telling anyone, I messaged Kelsey to let her know where I was.

Nic lived on an estate of pretty much identical mid-sixties town houses. I drove past and had to turn around as I'd missed it the first time. There was no car on the drive so I wasn't entirely certain anyone would be home. I double-checked the number before I knocked on the door. She had fussy net curtains but they had been pulled back a bit at the side of the window nearest the door. This was obviously Nic's sophisticated security system. I cupped my hands around my eyes and pushed my face against the glass. What I saw inside my made my stomach churn.

It was a shrine. The whole room was a shrine to Belinda Price. There was a life-sized cut-out of her next to the fireplace; on the walls were posters, magazine articles and photos of her. A couple were signed. One photo was very familiar – it was the one we had seen at Burntwood, except the girl who may or may not have been Nadiya had been crudely cut out so it looked as though it was just Nic and Belinda sharing an intimate moment. I felt completely chilled.

'I just got your call. I've been out getting a paper.'

I nearly headbutted the window in shock. I spun round guiltily to face Nic, who was holding a *Sunday Times*, a pint of milk and some Maltesers.

'I, er…' I couldn't get over the shock of what I'd seen in her lounge. The words just wouldn't come.

'You seen my lounge, then? I suppose you'll be wanting to talk about that. You coming in?'

I wasn't sure if I wanted to but I couldn't turn back now. I had to find out what was going on. I had told Kelsey if I wasn't in touch by three to send Jacob round. I took some small satisfaction in the fact that my abduction and possible murder would screw with his lunch plans with Kim. Death was a small price to pay, I felt.

I smiled brightly and said, 'Sure. I'm intrigued, I can tell you that!'

The hallway looked relatively normal, as did the kitchen where she led me. It was all a bit dated in 90s pine with terracotta tiles but it was clean and tidy. It was a lot more welcoming than Nadiya's fancy marble and slate. Nic flicked on the kettle and turned to face me. 'Look, Cherry. I know that this all looks a bit odd but you have to understand that Belinda was my best friend. I've always followed her career and collected bits and pieces. It makes me feel as though I'm in touch with her even though she's... she's... dead!' Her eyes reddened and started to fill up. She waved her hand uselessly in front of her face and dug around in her pocket for a tissue.

I reached across the table and gave her a hug. 'I understand, it must be really hard since you've been friends for so long.'

'Yes, I knew her before she was Belinda Price, famous television hostess. I knew her when she was just plain Lin.' She finished making the tea and picked up the mugs. We went into the lounge.

I walked over to *The Wizard of Oz* photo and pointed to the cut out bit. 'Who was the girl who played Dorothy?'

Nic looked confused. 'How do you know about that? Have you been, like, completely spying on me or just peering through my windows when I'm out of the house? Cos I'm trying not to make a fuss about that, Cherry, but I am quite shocked that you would behave that way.'

Oh no, I could easily see how it would look that way. 'No, no, it's nothing like that. I was at your old school yesterday with a family friend who was auditioning and I saw this photo in the hall of fame but there was a third girl. Short and cross-looking. I just wondered who she was, that's all.'

'That was Masha, Masha Konstantin.'

'And the woman there told me that Masha left under, er, difficult circumstances…'

'Yes, she just disappeared one morning. I mean, there was the accident first but then she left. Why? Do you think she killed Belinda?'

I wasn't sure. There was something here, I was sure of it, but something was missing. 'I don't know. What kind of accident?'

'Oh, she slipped and fell. Had to go to hospital and had only been back a few days when a taxi arrived and off she went.'

'Did you enjoy school?'

'Yes, I loved it. And once I was friends with Lin, I had a brilliant time. I just didn't want to be a dancer.'

'And what was Lin like at school?'

She frowned as if searching for the right words. 'She was very popular. She made you feel really special.'

I noticed her careful word choice and pressed a bit more. 'I bet she didn't like anyone else getting the limelight though, eh?'

Nic frowned and equivocated again. 'She was quite focused, you know. Wanted the best parts so she could get an agent. But she was very talented.'

'Was she friends with Masha?'

Nic paused as if caught out by my question. 'Not really, no.'

I could sense that there was more to it than this. I imagined the pretty, confident Belinda full of high self-esteem and how she might react to someone who lacked these things. How she might manipulate those weaknesses. I had to tread lightly here. Nic had a shrine to the woman. I opted for flattery as it had worked with Nic before.

'I bet you were a kind friend to Masha, though, weren't you?'

'Yes, I tried to be, it's just that…'

Gently, Cherry, I urged myself. 'Mmh hmm?'

'Well, Belinda wasn't always very nice to people who she thought might be rivals. You know?'

'Really, I'm surprised she even had rivals.'

'Well, no, she didn't really but she was… insecure, you know?'

I nodded and smiled in agreement. 'But nothing too unkind, though, surely?'

Nic frowned; she looked uncertain about continuing. I stayed quiet and left the question hanging, waiting for her to bite. Which she did. 'Well, there was this one time, actually, just before that show that the picture of the three of us came from. It was an end-of-year showcase where the agents, casting agents and producers come along and Lin, that's what everyone called Belinda, had so badly wanted to be Dorothy. Everyone expected her to be Dorothy but the teachers had cast Masha.'

I gently added, 'I bet Belinda was really put out about that.'

'Yes, she was furious. She used to call Masha names like Russian pig and Russian troll – you know, instead of Russian doll. So, this one time, we are about to go on and she gets this big tub of hair gel. So, I ought to say that the teacher has spent ages straightening Masha's hair and putting it in plaits so it looks really nice. You could tell Masha felt nice about it, she was smiling and that. And then Lin goes up to her with this gel and is, like, "Put some on your head now."'

'No! That's really mean. What did everyone else do?'

Nic bristled at this because she knew that my question was about her own part in this incident. 'Well, of course, we all tried to get Lin to stop it but she was very… determined and no one wanted to, er, you know, fall out with Lin.'

'And did Masha put the gel on her hair?'

'Yes, Lin told her if she didn't then she would force her to eat it and she'd be sick and unable to perform. So she had to perform with this gel dripping down her face and her neck, with a great big wet stain all down her frock. Like she was sweating or something. Good job they took the cast shots a few days before, really. We did all try to stop Lin, though. It wasn't like we all thought it was right. But she had this way. Would say things like, "Nicky, you're my very best friend, you know that, don't you?" and you wanted it to be true.'

I wasn't a fool. I'd been to school and seen what the popular girls who had the right make-up, shoes and school bag did to the fat girls, the girls with bad hair or spots or shoes bought with vouchers. Nic clearly idolised Belinda but I could imagine her as a bully. Indeed, wasn't that what the registrar had said when we asked about her? Nic's stock in trade was to sit quietly on the sidelines. I could picture her as Belinda's sidekick.

'Nic, do you think that there's any chance that Masha and Nadiya are the same person?'

'What?' She nearly dropped her tea in shock. 'No way. I mean, you have seen Nadiya, haven't you? She's tall and slim and graceful and Masha wasn't any of those things. Absolutely no way on Earth they are the same person. No way!'

She seemed pretty adamant and there wasn't much else to say on the matter. Beyond learning that Belinda was not a very nice person, which, to be fair, I'd already heard from at least two other sources, I still felt like I was stuck in a dead end. The whole Burntwood link had appeared to be a good lead but had gone absolutely nowhere. I thanked Nic for the tea and apologised again for my peeping Tom act.

Chapter Twenty-Three

I knew that I would have to give in sooner or later and catch up with my mum. So, on leaving Nic's house, I headed back towards Hutton with a view to dropping in on them before I went home. I had my strategy planned if she kicked off.

There was no need to knock since I'd been spotted the instant my car pulled into their close. The door flew open and my mum presented her cheek for a kiss. My dad was in the living room reading the *Daily Mail*, and on the coffee table, folded so the incriminating image was facing up, was the *Essex Chronicle*. My dad grunted some welcoming noises and Mum bustled off to make some tea. I decided to go for it.

'I see you've seen the results of my latest investigation.'

Mum shouted from the kitchen, 'Is that what they're calling it nowadays?'

And Dad added, 'He's certainly investigating what's under your dress, that's for sure!'

'Mike!' shouted Mum, outraged. 'There's no need to be crude about it.'

He shrugged. 'Just stating the facts, love, just stating the facts.'

I saw my chance. 'Well, yes, the facts are very important so that's why I wanted to let you both know that—'

My mum put a cup of tea and a London Cheesecake down next to me. 'It's OK, love, you don't have to explain yourselves to us. It's your life as so long as you're happy, we're happy. Aren't we, Mike?'

Dad glanced up from an article about how some bakeries were avoiding the term 'gingerbread man' in favour of the gender-neutral 'gingerbread person'. His face was a vision of outrage. 'Yes, yes, we're happy. Well, your mum's happy because everyone down the WI has been led to believe that that Jack Harrison is about to be her son-in-law.'

'Mike, don't overexaggerate. I only told Elaine-with-the-leg about it and she went spreading it round all the groups. Mexican Julie came up to me and told me she was going to cancel her holiday so she didn't miss the wedding. God knows what that Elaine told them.'

What was there to say to this? It was better than the telling-off I had expected for being seen cavorting on the front of the paper again but I guess if the person with whom your daughter was cavorting gave you bragging rights, it was different. I was shocked by my mum's double standards.

She had brought over tea for herself and my dad and was sitting down now. 'So, how's the investigation going? Are you any closer to finding out who killed Belinda and who's trying to bump off Nadiya?'

'Not really; I thought I'd found a good lead with this picture that showed Belinda, Nic and Nadiya at school together but everyone swears it's not her. And Jacob has got back with Kim Bolton.' I wasn't sure how this last bit had slipped out, but it was very hard for me to keep secrets from my mum.

'What? Plastic tits Kim Bolton? No way! I thought yous two were getting it all back on. Didn't we say, Mike, that it looked like it was all back on?'

'Yes, dear,' said Dad wearily.

'He was being so solicitous when he came round here, helping you to the car and that and then, all the time, he was planning on getting back with that big-boobed, scrawny… tramp!' The tea in her hand slopped around dangerously as she voiced her indignation. 'Well, he's not welcome round here again, I can tell you.'

'Thanks, Mum,' I sighed, 'I need to just focus on this case now and not worry about men. I don't know what to do, though.'

Dad looked up from his paper. 'Have you shown this Nadiya the picture that you thought was her?'

'No.'

Mum joined in, 'Why not? Maybe there's a reason for Nic to hide the fact that they were at school together, eh? Something incriminating?'

They had a point. Maybe this wasn't such a dead end after all.

'Yes, I can see that. OK, I'll try her. Thanks, Mum.' I drained the last of my tea and stood up to leave.

'Oh, I didn't expect you to leave right away. I was going to show you my pictures from the craft fair I went to last week. One of Margaret's things for the dogs' home. She'd knitted ninety-seven bobble hats for Chocolate Oranges.'

'Why?'

'Well, it looks nice – people are into that sort of thing.'

'A Chocolate Orange with a bobble hat?'

'Don't be pulling that face, Cherry Hinton, it's what everyone has got for Christmas.'

I saw my dad roll his eyes.

'Sounds great, Mum. I look forward to receiving my Chocolate Orange with winter attire. On that note, I'm going to go and catch Nadiya. See you both later.'

I gave them each a hug and a kiss and made my escape before my mum could find the hilarious chain email she'd been sent by Elaine-with-the-leg.

Chapter Twenty-Four

I drove as quickly as I could round to Shenfield Green in a bid to catch Nadiya at home. I was hoping that she was in a more pleasant mood than when I'd last seen her. The police car had gone from outside her house but I was fervently hoping that she was still being security conscious.

I knocked on the door and waited for ages. Finally, I heard footsteps and the grinding of locks and bolts. The door swung open and there she was, looking as well as when I had seen her on that first day in the green room. She even looked vaguely pleased to see me.

'Ah, Cherry. Hello, it is you. Come in.'

She stepped aside and I walked into the hallway. Someone had erected a massive Christmas tree and decorated it with tasteful blue and gold decorations which all matched. It reminded me that I needed to do mine at home.

There had also been a lot of tidying done. The boxes, bags and packaging material had all disappeared and there were only a few items and bunches of flowers on the hall table. I must have looked at it in surprise as she said, 'I have had a lot of time on my hands to tidy up. See, I am not a messy person after all. Come through.'

We went through into her enviable kitchen where a pot of coffee was brewing in a machine. She had a fancy box of mince pies on the counter, which she opened and offered me. I hesitated slightly and she said, 'It is fine. I ordered them myself and they were completely sealed when they arrived. Also I have eaten two.'

I smiled. 'Well, I'll trust them, then. They look delicious. Thank you.'

She poured us each a coffee and then sat down on the stool opposite. 'So, Cherry, how is your investigation going?'

'Well, I'm glad you asked. I wanted to talk to you about this photo.' I showed her the shot of the black-and-white photo from Burntwood. I watched her face carefully – not a flicker.

She raised one eyebrow. 'I see poor Belinda as a child and is that... Nicky Johnston? I do not know who Dorothy is. Is this your investigation?'

I'm sure she didn't mean to sound quite as scathing and sarcastic as she did but nevertheless, it irked me intensely.

'Well, yes. I had thought that maybe Dorothy could be you.'

'Me?' She sounded horrified.

'Yes, I mean, if you pushed back the fringe and lost a few pounds.'

'This is not me. I cannot believe that you would say such a thing. I wanted you to find out who has been trying to harm me, not show me pictures from the past and accuse me of being frizzy-haired little girl. And besides, I am sure this was taken before I came into the country.'

She looked completely outraged, like I'd just compared her to a picture of a poo in a carrier bag. I felt it was a bit of an overreaction. 'Look, Nadiya, I'm sorry. I didn't mean to upset you. I just thought that if there was a connection between you from the past then maybe someone had a reason to kill both you and Belinda.'

She scoffed at this but seemed a bit mollified. 'It is Nicky Johnston you should talk to. She always behaved strangely around Belinda.'

'Like strangely how?'

She took a sip of black coffee and thought about it. 'Like she kind of loved her and hated her at the same time. You know, if Detective Stow left you for someone else you would both love him and hate him at the same time.'

As examples went, it felt a bit too near the knuckle for this to be something she'd just made up. I didn't want to fall out with her so I let it slide. 'Yes, I do know what you mean. Are you saying that you think Nic was in love, like, romantically, with Belinda?'

'Yes, maybe, perhaps more like a fan and their superstar. I see it in the way some people look at me. Like you, Cherry.'

I wasn't sure where this was going. 'Er, what do you mean?'

'When you first saw me, you looked at me like Nicky always looked at Belinda. You don't do it so much any more.'

'I'm not some adoring fan, Nadiya. I'm a professional.' I didn't remember gaping at her like a fool but I probably had, knowing me.

'No, you did and your friend. You tried better to hide it.'

'No, I don't think I did.'

She shrugged. 'It's no matter, Cherry. I am used to it. It is not easy being as beautiful as me and attracting men and women.'

I was starting to wonder if she could actually be any more arrogant than she was already. It turned out she could.

'So when you show me this picture of this little Russian troll, you see how I can become angry, yes?'

Yes, I did see but I also saw very clearly that she was lying about something, whether it was her in the picture or someone else. The atmosphere in the room changed slightly and I think she sensed that she had said something wrong. Her eyes glanced around warily and I suddenly felt cold. A voice in my gut told me to go and go quickly.

I drained my coffee and realised with some discomfort that I'd had far too many hot drinks that day and was busting for the toilet. I wanted to leave as soon as I could because I felt very scared. Nadiya Slipchenko was a liar and I didn't want to be in her home for one moment longer. However, I also knew that on a Sunday afternoon in Shenfield, there was nowhere to go to the loo. Reluctantly, I asked if she could tell me where it was and I scuttled off into a downstairs bathroom that was the size of my lounge. I went as quickly as I could while texting Kelsey and Jacob in case anything happened to me before I could leave the house.

I stepped out of the room cautiously and collected up my things from the kitchen counter. For some reason I couldn't explain rationally, I was gripped by a fear of Nadiya and what she might do. I dithered so that Nadiya was walking in front of me and I could feel my heart pounding in my chest. I kept expecting her to turn around and confront me or for someone to appear from one of the numerous downstairs rooms and grab me but no, I made it unscathed to the front door.

With only the briefest of goodbyes, I nearly ran to my car. I locked all the doors after checking the back seat and only when I pulled out of her road and on to the Broadway did I release the breath I had been holding for the last couple of minutes. I checked the time – it was nearly four and getting dark so I decided that I'd done enough for the day and headed home.

I noticed the car in my mirror as it was doing that thing where someone wants to overtake: driving up close and sort of pulling out a bit. Alexander Lane was narrow, dark and bendy so a silly choice for trying to overtake on anyway. I thought to myself that they were obviously not local as they would know that the Chelmsford Road was at the end and then they could easily overtake.

However, I was so distracted by the car behind me that I didn't see the car in front appear from what was like literally nowhere. Just before we got to the back of my old school, the car in front slammed on their brakes and turned so they were taking up the whole road. Adrenaline surged through my body and my hands started to shake. Obviously, I pumped the brakes and skidded to a halt, millimetres away from smashing into the side of the car. It was only when I realised the car behind had adopted a similar blocking position on the road that it occurred to me that this was a set-up and I was probably going to die.

You'd have thought after watching loads of action movies, I'd know exactly what to do if I were confronted by Russian gangsters on a dark country lane. I would use my jujitsu skills or get out my handy gun or acquire super-human speed and run away. I did none of those things; I simply froze with fear. I couldn't even get my hands off the steering wheel. My knees and jaw shook uncontrollably as I waited for something to happen.

Nobody moved in the car behind but the driver and passenger got out of the car in front. The driver was massive. He wore a black anorak and a black balaclava; in his hand he held a gun. A big gun like you see the police with at Heathrow Airport. It looked like a serious gun for shooting people with. I struggled to breathe. The passenger, much to my horror, was a guy wearing a *Scream* mask. My brain struggled to compute what was going on. Had I been found by Ugroza?

The driver rapped his knuckles on the window but my hands were frozen to the steering wheel. He knocked again and shouted but I couldn't move. Then he smashed the window with the butt of his gun. Glass flew everywhere – in my face, in my hair, my hands, my lap. I was panting with fear. Rough hands dragged me out of the car and to my feet.

I heard my voice say, 'Please, please.'

Then Scream spoke. 'Shut up and listen; we don't have much time.'

I did as he said.

'You need to stop asking questions about Burntwood Academy, yes?'

I said nothing.

The driver, who was holding me up, shook me a little bit to get a response. I squeaked, 'Yes.'

'You put everyone in danger with your questions, you understand?'

I didn't need shaking. 'No.'

'What?'

'No. You asked if I understood and I said no.'

Scream Mask looked over my shoulder at the driver – I flinched away as I thought that this was the moment he would order my execution. Then he said, 'I told you that this is what she is like. She doesn't do scared.'

Did he mean me? The woman who most certainly would have soiled herself had she not had a wee a few minutes before. Was there a problem that I wasn't scared enough?

'I *am* scared, I'm really scared.'

'Then you are meant to agree with everything I say! That's how it works.'

The driver said in a thick London accent, 'I can 'it 'er if you like.'

I gabbled, panicking, 'No, please don't hit me. I agree, I understand. I totally understand that I shouldn't ask about the picture because… because it *is* Nadiya, isn't it?'

Scream Mask turned to me. 'Just stop asking questions. This is a warning to stop asking questions. Do you understand?'

I nodded vigorously. I was starting to feel dizzy from my shallow panting breaths. The cold night air hurt the cuts on my face and head. I wondered why there were no other cars on the road. Surely someone would have come along by now?

The driver said, 'Oi, Lexi, do you want me to hit her now?'

Lexi? Of course it was. How did I not notice this before?

He turned away and leaned over the bonnet of my car, shaking his head. And then I remembered the thing that I'd been trying to unstick since I'd heard it. Alexi had told me that to keep his sister safe, he had sent her away to school in England *and she had hated it*. Without giving it too much thought I said, 'Oh, I totally understand *now*. Nadiya, or *Masha*, was your sister. You sent her to Burntwood but she hated it so you brought her home and then sent her back again but to Damien Spiritwind? Is that it?'

The driver, whose leather-gloved hands were cutting in to my upper arms, muttered, 'She's good, though, isn't she, even if she doesn't know when to shut up.'

Alexi removed the pointless *Scream* mask and scowled deeply at me. I noticed that he looked all sweaty in the thin light from his car's interior. 'Yes, all of this is true. She did not fit in. She saw how I had worked to transform myself and did the same. But your questions must stop now. You put us both in danger – Nadiya must not be linked with the name Masha Konstantin and neither must I. I thought you understood the dangers of Ugroza last time we spoke.'

I was starting to think that he wasn't going to kill me after all and some feeling came back into my legs. 'I do understand but what I don't understand is all this – you've broken my car window.'

The driver, who had eased up somewhat, resumed his grip on me and twisted my collar at the back. Alexi came up close and spoke with a quiet anger. 'I want you to understand how dangerous your questions are. My sister has nearly died four times at the hand of some maniac and now you are drawing attention to her past. Next time, it won't be my friend Simon with a replica firearm. If Ugroza think you are anything at all to do with our disappearance, you will be gunned down in your shop. No mercy, no chittychat. Take this as a warning to shut up and find out who is killing her.'

In the distance, I heard a shout. 'Cherry?'

The car blocking me from behind suddenly started up and Alexi looked panicked.

I tried to twist round and see who had come to rescue me but at the same time, Alexi signalled to Simon, who raised the butt of his gun and smashed me in the face with it.

The pain was simply indescribable; it was like my whole body was a sort of twisting tornado of agony and my nose was like the eye of the storm where the pain-energy radiated from. I instinctively reached up to hold it but all that was there was a hot pulpy mass of slippery wet blood. In that moment, it felt like I had a hole in the middle of my face. I cupped my hands pointlessly over my face and tried to breathe through my mouth and not panic. Both cars had sped off and, for a moment, I stood simply swaying in the middle of the road, not sure what to do. Footsteps clattered on the road behind me and I turned around.

Jacob let out a terrible, high-pitched scream. 'Cherry, oh my God.'

I went to reply and realised that I actually couldn't talk and breathe at the same time. I just stood there with my hands over my face.

Jacob brought his phone to his ear and kept his focus on me. 'Yes, I need an ambulance and the back-up unit right away. On Alexander Lane – closer to the Chelmsford Road end. One female victim. Still conscious.'

He guided me very gently over to the passenger seat of my car, where there was no glass, and pulled off his coat. He draped it over my shoulders and helped to lower me into the seat. 'It's OK, don't try to speak. Just sit still and keep breathing. The ambulance will be here soon. I can't believe they hit you.' He waffled on, patting the back of my hand, and it occurred to me that this typified my relationship with Jacob. He was always just a bit too late. Why hadn't he arrived when Alexi and his cronies had tried to box me in with their cars? Why did he arrive when my car had been smashed, just in time to see me get smacked in the face with a very convincing replica firearm?

Chapter Twenty-Five

Once the paramedics had arrived and dosed me up with painkillers, I didn't have much memory of what happened after that. It did transpire that it wasn't as bad as I had initially thought, as it was quite a clean break. It was the glass from the smashed window that had caused more problems as quite a lot had embedded itself in my scalp and neck. I stayed in overnight as they were worried about clots in my nose causing trouble with breathing.

Jacob had briefly appeared with Ben, one of his constables, to ask me about the incident and I had recounted what happened to the best of my ability to recall. Since I hadn't seen anyone's face apart from Alexi's and I hadn't seen any number plates or car models, I wasn't able to be of much use. I did mention Simon to them and Ben made a note of it and shrugged.

'Do you think that this picture had something to do with Nadiya's, accidents then?' asked Jacob.

'Maybe Belinda knew it was her and was blackmailing her or maybe Belinda was trying to kill her. I don't know. It's all such a muddle. There must be a connection.'

'Or maybe not,' he suggested. 'Maybe Belinda's murder and Nadiya's attempted murder are two separate crimes committed by two different people.'

My head was feeling fuzzy and sore. 'But what is the motive? What does anyone have to gain by harming either of them? Is there money somewhere?'

Jacob shook his head. 'No, we looked at that. There's nothing for anyone. I think Belinda's sister gets her house but that's about it. Nadiya has nothing, hardly any savings. There's something we're missing.'

I could barely keep my eyes open. Jacob glanced at me and then at Ben, who took the hint immediately. Clearing his throat, he said, 'Well, I promised Audrey a Chinese tonight so if there's nothing else you need, boss…?'

Jacob replied with studied casualness, 'No, you're OK, go ahead, enjoy your prawn wontons.'

Ben left hurriedly and closed the door behind him. We both waited a moment or two and then I said, 'Jacob, it's OK. You don't have to stay. You did your best.' I was doing *my* best to rewrite my story. Him hanging around looking all sexy and sympathetic while blood clots formed in my nose was not the way forward for either of us.

'I just wanted to say that I was sorry I didn't take what you had to say seriously and I'm sorry you've got hurt again.'

I tried my best to smile beneath the dressings. 'Unless you've been disguising yourself as a thug and a poisoner, none of those things are your fault. There's no need to apologise. Now go.'

'Well, if you're sure. Kim's back at my flat waiting so I guess I'd better go back and see her.'

'Cool. Bye.' Thankfully the bandages muffled the sound of my heart breaking all over again as he left me in my hot little hospital room. I closed my eyes and was just drifting off on a wave of morphine when I heard a huge commotion outside. My eyes shot open and my heart rate rocketed. Had Ugroza come to finish the job Alexi started?

I heard a familiar voice say, 'I'm not here to visit, am I? She's my lesbian wife and I demand to see her right now.' And then the door banged open and Kelsey was there clutching a bag of grapes and a bottle of Lucozade. She went on, 'Oh, my darling Cherry, my darling lesbian wife. Thank goodness you're alive,' in possibly the world's most stilted and artificial voice. She had definitely not missed her calling as an actress.

The ward sister looked on with disapproval and narrow-eyed suspicion. 'Just ten minutes, then. The policeman said no visitors at all.' She shut the door with a snappy click.

Kelsey straightened herself from her prostrate position across me on the bed. 'Mate. I cannot believe what's happened. Look at the state of your face.'

'I actually don't want to, I'm too scared that I might look like the Elephant Man's wife.'

Kelsey looked and nodded. 'Yeah, I'm not gunna lie to you, babe. You look fucking awful. Your mum is gunna go off her head when she sees you.'

'Which is why I've not told her I'm here.'

'What? If there's one thing even more designed to make Carol go off her head than seeing you with your face smacked in, it's not knowing you had your face smacked in. You're a brave woman, Cherry Hinton.'

'Yeah, well, I'm hoping for the sympathy vote.' I leant back weakly into my sympathy-grabbing pose.

'Anyways, I want to hear all about it and then you can ask me for my big revelation. OK? Can I take a picture for my followers?' She slipped her phone out of her silver puffa jacket and held it aloft.

'No, Kelsey, I don't want nine thousand people seeing what I look like when I've been beaten up by Russian gangsters. Come on, give a girl some dignity.'

'Actually, it's five hundred thousand and seventy-two.'

'What is?'

'My followers.'

'Kelsey! Shall we stick with the important bits of the conversation, eh?'

She pulled a sulky pout and put her phone down. 'Fine. Go on, then – tell me what happened.'

'So, I went to Nic's house and she wasn't there so I had a sneaky peek through the curtains…'

'Nice, like your style, Chezza.' She popped a grape in her mouth and chomped loudly on it.

'Where I found one room set up entirely as a shrine to Belinda Price.'

'No fucking way.' She was loving it.

'Yes fucking way. Like so weird on so many levels and the photo was there again but with Masha cut off. So anyways, I was getting well into how weird it was when Nic only fucking caught me.'

Kelsey gasped and helped herself to some more grapes. 'Noooo. Then what?'

'Well, she was surprisingly OK about it. Invited me in, denied Masha was Nadiya and basically told me that Belinda was a big bitch at school. Apparently she was especially horrible to Masha – called her all sorts of names like Russian troll and that but Nic still loved her.'

Kelsey scoffed some more grapes. 'That's helpful, I guess. Then what?'

'Then I went to see Mum and Dad.'

'Was your mum totally vexed about Jack Harrison?'

I shook my head. 'No, she thinks he's sexy and I should do what makes me happy. I think it's because her mates down the WI like him.'

'Yeah, and he's not dead Kenny.' She shrugged with regret. We'd both been fond of Kenny when we were at school with him. He'd been an excellent Kenickie to Felix's Danny Zuko. Kenny had been my first boyfriend and, sadly, Kenny's murder had been my first case.

I sighed. 'Poor Kenny. This is true. Anyways, they're like, "Why don't you ask Nadiya about the photo?" So I did and that's when the shit hit the fan.'

'How?' Not only had the phone gone down now but she'd taken both her hand and her glance off it.

'So, Nadiya, like, *totally* lies. First thing she does is she gives it that it's not her.'

'OK, pretty standard response for an amateur liar,' she said scornfully.

'But then she calls Nic "Nicky" and who is the only other person we've heard call Nic "Nicky"—'

In unison, we chorused, 'Cheap Suit!'

'And then, bearing in mind, I've said nothing about this other girl in the photo, she calls her a "Russian troll".'

Kelsey's eyes went wide. 'And you just said that's what Belinda used to call her?' And then how would she know that the girl in the picture was Russian or whatever just by looking at her? She must have at least been there.'

'Exactly. And then the room went all weird. Like the vibe changed and she behaved like she knew I knew and I got all freaked out and left.'

Kelsey frowned and went to speak but the door banged open.

'I told you, she's my mum!'

Kaleese.

The nurse, who had clearly had a long, tiring day and was also not in the mood for Kaleese's shit, replied dryly, 'Which of this lesbian couple is your mother?'

To which Kaleese wokely responded, 'I can't believe you even asked me that. Have you had no inclusivity training or nothing? They are both my mother. I bet you wouldn't ask a kid that if it was a heteronormative couple, would you?'

Kelsey muttered under her breath, 'Well, it'd be pretty fucking obvious which one was the mother in that case, wouldn't it?'

The nurse tutted and said, 'Ten minutes only. Your *mother* has a very serious injury.'

Kaleese was dressed head to toe in leisurewear encrusted with pink sparkles and massive trainers. She was holding a copy of *Close-Up* magazine, which she put next to the bed apologetically. It had clearly been read several times and was dated from last June. 'It was all I had to bring for you to read. Either that or *An Inspector Fucking Calls*, which I never gave back to school when I left. What a waste of time that was. Like, is socialism even a real thing?'

She and Kelsey rolled their eyes at each other and I closed mine briefly. They were hard work as a pair.

'So, Cherry,' began Kaleese, 'I've got a fucking mental story for you. I was gunna call yesterday but I thought you might have had a big one Saturday so I waited and then I was too late.'

'Leese, get on with it. Cherry's had a terrible injury. Look at the state of her!'

'Sick! Can I take a photo?'

'No, have some sensitivity for the poor woman.' Oh the irony.

'Kaleese, please, tell me the story.'

'Right, so I've just done my first audition, which is the group dance thing, so I'm like sitting down and there's this older girl there who's in the upper sixth and we can, like, ask her questions and stuff and so, like, everyone is giving it, "Is it dead hard?", "Is everyone friends?", that sort of shit, so I ask what happens if you get injured and that, do you lose your place at the school if you have to take time out for physio and that? And the main sixth form one goes in an all posh voice, "That's a matter for the governors and is dealt with on a case-by-case basis" and then there's this other one who came from a state school for sixth form who I reckon is there to make us chavs feel a bit better and she gives it, "Well, that Belinda Price who's dead off the telly once threw another girl down the stairs and she broke her ankle in three places and had to leave."'

There is silence as we try to process Kaleese's somewhat complex narrative. She could have given James Joyce a run for his money in terms of density, I reckoned. I get there first. 'Did she tell you what the girl with the leg injury was called?'

Kaleese paused and frowned. Kelsey looked as though she was going to throttle her or something. 'Come on, think harder!'

Kalesse shrugged. 'I dunno, something Russian.'

'Was it Masha Konstantin?' I asked.

Kaleese shrugged again. 'Yeah that sounds like it.'

'So, Belinda Price throws Masha down the stairs, Masha leaves; never to be seen again. It's got to be her.'

Kaleese was confused. 'Who? Who has it got to be?'

Kelsey is pretty quick to follow me. 'Masha has an ankle injury and Nadiya also has an ankle injury that ended her competing career four years ago.'

Kaleese looked confused. 'So is Masha Nadiya?'

'Yes!' I almost shout. 'Yes, she bloody well is.'

Chapter Twenty-Six

Hinton in Brutal Attack

By Julia Scofield

Cherry Hinton, former star of The Caravan of Love, *was the victim of a brutal beating in a terrifying gangland attack. She was found in the road by crime-fighting superhero DS Jacob Stow and rushed to Harold Wood Hospital for urgent treatment. This is Hinton's second hospital stay in a matter of weeks. It seems someone really does not want Cherry to get to the bottom of this terrifying case. A spokeswoman for Hinton said, 'Cherry has been dead brave and she will sort out this crime if it's the last thing she does.' Let's hope that this is not the last thing she does.*

'Well, she must have had someone in the hospital taking your photo. I can't believe the cheek of the woman. It would have been better if she'd used the one with the pants that she always gets out whenever you do anything. I mean, at least you look attractive in that.'

I sighed. Mums really know how to perk you up when you're feeling low. I was supposed to be recuperating on the settee. Weird orange ming dripped out of my nose on an intermittent basis and I was still too scared to look closely at my face. The district nurse had replaced my heavy-duty bandages with some lighter gauze and everything felt tight and itchy, which I was assured was a good thing. I was doing my best to stay still, have restful thoughts and keep my fluids up. I was itching to get better so I could call Chris Gordon and claim my cash. Poor D'arcy had been left to her own devices in the shop again but Mum had been making surprise spot checks and had commented on how clean she had been keeping everything so I wasn't overly concerned.

After several text exchanges and one phone call, Chris and I set a date to recall the cast of the show back to the studio for a 'closure briefing'. The show had ultimately been axed for this season in light of Belinda's death and Alexi's strange disappearance. Chris had been hit hard for fees and insurance and I'd heard on the grapevine (via one of Kelsey's ladies) that Leon Solent had demanded a huge sum for loss of earnings after sponsoring the show and had, miraculously, been given it. I was sure Leon's methods had been very persuasive.

The day finally came and my face was pretty much back to normal. As my mum had pointed out, it wasn't like I was a supermodel or anything so my slightly bumpy nose and livid scar weren't going to affect me in the long run. I still felt ugly and was grateful to Kelsey, who came over and applied a truckload of make-up to make me look a bit more like I used to. I had borrowed a pale pink trouser suit which I wore with a slinky black shirt. I thought I looked good or at least like the best version of me.

I drove myself, Kelsey and Kaleese. Essentially, everyone who was there on the day Belinda was killed had been invited along with Jacob and his team. I had pre-warned him that some of my ideas were purely speculative but there were other things I had evidence for. He had tutted on the phone but since he had not come up with anything close to a solution, I knew he would turn up.

I hadn't, however, prepared myself emotionally for him turning up with Kim on his arm. We met them in the car park. I hissed at Kelsey and Kaleese to say nothing as they walked towards us.

Jacob had on an awkward, fake smile. I'm sure we were the last people he wanted to encounter in the car park too. 'Hi, Cherry, you remember Kim, don't you?'

Kim smiled vacantly at me. 'No, I don't think so. Are you that one off the telly?'

I smiled back as genuinely as I could. 'Depends what you've been watching, really. Not lately, though.'

Kaleese, who was incapable of following orders, said, 'She was on *The Caravan of Love* and she is an investigator.'

Kim looked confused. Maybe Kaleese had used too many long words at once for Kim to process. I was praying that Jacob would keep things moving along since we were all headed in the same direction but no, Kim seemed intent on standing still and looking at me.

She smiled again. 'You're Cherry Hinton. I know what I wanted to ask you: would you come on *Watch My Ex Having Sex* with me and Jakey?'

I looked at Jacob, who had buried his face in his hands. I heard an outraged intake of breath behind me.

'You did not just fucking say that!' shouted Kelsey. 'Look at her, she's just got back to work after recovering from being smacked in the face by some crazy Russian.'

'Crazy Ukrainian's mate,' I said quietly but no one paid any attention.

'Yeah,' chipped in Kaleese, 'and what does she wanna watch you and Jacob having sex for? She's just got over food poisoning, she doesn't wanna be puking up all over again.' Kaleese had clearly been in training with her sister.

Kim looked shocked. Like, genuinely shocked. As if she'd expected me to say 'Yes please' or 'Thank you very much'. She stood there awkwardly and gazed up at Jacob. Who, unsurprisingly, had moved ever so slightly away from her.

Because she was such an idiot with no ability to read the situation, Kim tried again. 'It's just that I've been approached by Chris Gordon and he's prepared to offer us all a lot of money. I mean obviously me and Jakey more since we'd actually be having the sex but he said you could have three thousand pounds.' She giggled and nodded at me eagerly. 'I mean that's not bad, is it?'

There was a painful silence where everyone stood looking at her.

I said, 'Even if my life depended on it, I would rather die than watch you and Jacob having sex. In fact, I'd rather masturbate on live TV with two bananas than watch you two going at it.'

Kim looked at me with a disgusted expression on her face, swerved around where I was standing and, presumably, started walking towards the doors of the studio.

Jacob watched her go and tried to rescue the situation. 'Cherry, look, sorry, Kim's got a bit ahead of herself and overstepped the mark.'

'Yeah, you could say that.' I was actually lost for words.

Jacob tried again. 'This really wasn't my idea. You know I—'

He was interrupted by banshee-like screaming from Kim. I turned around to discover that Kim had tried to push past

Kelsey and had had a handful of hair extensions whipped out by Kaleese, who dropped them guiltily as we turned around.

'That's fucking assault, that is. She pushed me,' cried Kelsey indignantly.

Kim was just screaming, 'My hair, my fucking hair, that skank just pulled out my hair.'

'Who are you calling skank? I've seen more realistic hair on a fucking Barbie,' replied Kaleese.

'Ladies,' shouted Jacob, which shut everyone up. 'Nobody is going to be watching anyone have sex. Can we all just go inside now and leave each other alone. I would hate to have to look into assault charges.'

As they walked off ahead of us, I could have sworn I heard Kim say, 'But why would she need two bananas?'

We hung back a bit, since we had to pick our way carefully across the car park; both Kaleese and Kelsey were wearing stiletto boots and wanted to avoid the potholes and speed bumps. When we finally tottered into the studio, we were met with a strange sight.

Chris Gordon, who liked a bit of the theatrical as much as I did, had got everyone sitting down in two rows. They looked like expectant schoolchildren and I got a cheeky wink from Jack, which made me feel a bit more cheerful. There was quite a festive atmosphere and a few of the contestants were clutching cans of cocktails. I was suddenly aware that I was about to crush the spirit out of the room.

Chris came over to us and spoke to me in a low voice. 'Can I just double-check some bits with you?'

I waved the girls on and they rushed over to be the one who got to sit next to Jack Harrison. 'Yes, go on, what is it?'

'If this goes the way you explained it to me, I pay what we agreed?'

'Yes, that's right,' I said tentatively.

When we had spoken a few days before, Chris hadn't told me what my end of the deal was. To be fair to him, he had kept his word and organised this really quickly.

'OK, well, I've had a think and what I want from you—'

'Please don't say *Watch My Ex*; literally anything but that.'

He laughed. 'I take it Kim's already mentioned that, then? No, I'm not stupid, Cherry. As much as I'd like to see that, I do have some sort of moral code.'

I scoffed at that but smiled at the same time. Was it possible that I was growing slightly fond of Chris Gordon? 'Go on, then, what do you want?'

'I'd like you to front a docu-drama about what happened. We'll get someone else to play you and you can, like, introduce it and obviously help with the script. I'm gunna call it *Murder on the Dancefloor* and it'll be a one-off special.'

I quite liked the sound of that. 'Yeah, OK, are you going to find some stunning actress to play me?' I said lightly.

To which he responded, 'Don't be fucking stupid, Cherry, we want it to be slightly realistic!'

I speedily reviewed my fond feelings and let Chris begin the proceedings.

He cleared his throat and clapped his hands together. The chatter stopped and he began, 'So as you are all aware, today is a chance for us all to get some closure on what happened here – the terrible accidents that happened to Nadiya and, of course, the murder of Belinda. As you know, Cherry was employed by me to initially protect Nadiya from the dangers she perceived and then after Belinda's murder her role has shifted slightly to consult with the police. However, we are here this afternoon to hear about Cherry's findings and leave somewhat lighter of heart. Over to you, Cherry.' He got a semi-ironic smattering of applause from the drag queen presenters of the spin-off show, Gloria Serection and Fanny Batter, who were swigging cans of mojito in the back row.

He acknowledged this with a camp little wave and sat down.

With slightly shaky legs, I took the floor. 'So, let's start at the very beginning—'

I was interrupted by Gloria and Fanny singing, 'It's a very good place to start' from *The Sound of Music*. I saw Jacob turn around and shush them and he was rewarded with a big 'Oooh'.

A little unnerved, I continued, 'There were three accidents – Alexi throws a real knife and it only misses Nadiya by millimetres, a rogue camera escapes its tracks and nearly runs down Felix and Nadiya as they rehearse and a hook falls from the ceiling as Kelsey and I watch Nadiya warming up. Horrible accidents that, at the very least, would have injured Nadiya or could have killed her. At each of these accidents, five people are present. Sometimes there are more but these five are the only ones who are there each time. Who are those five people?'

I was interrupted again by Gloria and Fanny, who called out, 'They're behind you!', pantomime style.

Kelsey, who I'm sure had kept quiet up until this point because she was afraid of them, shouted, 'Oi, pipe down or go home!'

She too was responded to with a big 'Oooh!'

I didn't remember any of my literary detective heroes having these problems during the big final denouement. Channelling a bit of Miss Marple, I said loudly, 'Firstly, we have Felix Stow, the reputable MP for Brentwood North, but what is he hiding about his relationship with Nadiya…'

Felix spluttered, 'I told you before, I'd rather have sex with my own wife than her!'

Nadiya looked more deeply offended by this than she had a right to. 'That is not what you said when you took me to Marygreen Manor and made love to me all night long. You said I was the best you'd ever had.'

'Oh, don't worry, love,' I called, 'he says that to all the girls!' Perhaps I had more in common with Gloria and Fanny than I did Miss Marple. There was some smirking from the group and I noticed that even Jacob chuckled at this a little bit.

Felix had nothing to say. He sat back down again. I took it then that Nadiya had been telling the truth. Once again, I pondered on how deeply unlikeable Felix Stow was. I was glad I'd said what I did about his sexual prowess.

I pressed on. 'Then there is the mysterious Alexi Slipchenko, Nadiya's ex-boyfriend, except I have now discovered that he is none other than Nadiya's beloved older brother.'

'Euurgh. He was sleeping with his *sister?*' asked Kaleese.

I quickly interjected, 'Um, no, he wasn't. They just pretended so they could live together without being detected. At least, that's what I'm guessing. Nadiya, want to confirm that for us?'

She looked at me with pure loathing. 'Yes, he was my brother and no I did not have sex with him.' She spat out the words coldly.

I continued. 'So, on the face of it, Alexi has no reason to harm his own sister. In fact, he has spent most of his life trying to care for his sister. What about suspect number three? Damien Spiritwind. Alexi trusted Damien to care for his sixteen-year-old sister and what does Damien do? He becomes her lover to teach her the true meaning of dance. Is she definitely sixteen at the time? Does Nadiya carry a secret that could topple the whole Spiritwind Dance Empire? What would all the dance mums say if they discovered that the teacher slept with underaged students? Hmmm. She already sued for loss of earnings and settled out of court. Damien Spiritwind has plenty of reason to want Nadiya dead.'

'This is ridiculous, I'm leaving,' declared Damien, getting up out of his chair.

PC Ben Fleet was over pretty quick. 'Sit down, sir. No one is permitted to leave.'

'Then we turn to Nic Johnston' – I was getting into my stride now after the earlier interruptions – 'the jaunty leader of the band, who, it transpires, went to school with both Belinda and Nadiya. Were they friends at school or did Nadiya stand in the way of your relationship with Belinda?'

Nic frowned at this and shook her head. No dramatic response from her.

'And then we have Belinda herself. Five would-be murderers, but which one is it? None of them seemed to have a compelling enough reason to want Nadiya dead and, if they did, was a series of increasingly bizarre accidents their way of operating?'

I tried to create a dramatic pause but Kaleese, probably overexcited by the whole situation, called out, 'Clearly not because you're gonna make a big reveal!'

It was a bit spoilt now but I went for it. 'But then I realised that there was someone I'd forgotten. Someone who had also been present when Belinda was murdered and when I nearly died. Who was there every time?'

Kelsey half stood, like someone who had seen the light at an evangelical church event. 'Nadiya!'

'Exactly. Thank you, Kelsey. Nadiya was present during every accident and during Belinda's murder.'

'What is it you are trying to say?' cried Nadiya, her face a mask of anger.

'I'm trying to say what should have been glaringly obvious from the start. It was you! You staged the accidents and you killed Belinda. Your own brother gave me the clue when he said that if he was trying to kill you, he would cut your throat in bed. Who would bother with these quite frankly amateurish methods? Even my mum noticed that the only part of the whole thing which worked was Belinda being shot.'

Nadiya looked disgusted. 'And why? Why would I want to harm myself and kill Belinda?'

'You had no intention of harming yourself – you wanted Belinda's shooting to be taken as a crime directed at you. So we would all waste our time chasing shady Russians, dodgy dance teachers and sleazy politicians. So nobody would notice that Belinda Price was dead. Which we did.'

I walked towards where she was sitting, letting all my frustration out as I spoke, 'Oh, how clever you must have thought you were! Watching me pursuing Ugroza, getting poisoned and hit in the face by your brother's shady associate. Just out of interest, Nadiya, who did deliver those chocolates in the green box?'

A voice from the second row said, 'What, those fancy ones in the green box? That was me.'

Everyone craned around to see who was speaking. Jack Harrison. I was shocked. He seemed like a nice man and why would he not try to hide his face?

Jack continued, 'I mean, she asked me to and gave me the chocolates and everything. Just told me to drop them off at some point during the day. It was no big deal. Was it?'

He must have realised by the look on my face that it probably was a big deal because he added a sort of half-hearted, 'Sorry, didn't realise it was anything. No one asked, you see.'

Inside, I was fuming, not at Jack but at Jacob, who could have quite easily 'asked' after I spotted the cycling suit at Jack's house but chose to ignore me instead. It would certainly have saved me a whole load of hassle and a broken nose. But this was not the moment to be distracted by angry thoughts about Jacob.

I continued. 'But, Nadiya, you were not clever enough, though. There's only one person in this room who hated Belinda Price with a strong enough passion to kill her and that was *you*. She cost you your career and your dreams at Burntwood, didn't she?'

Nadiya stood up, almost as if she were relieved. It simply came pouring out of her. 'Yes, yes, she did and she deserved to die. She was a cruel, evil bully and my one regret is that she never knew what killed her. I was a stranger, I was fourteen, on the run from people who threatened to kill my whole family and she tormented me day and night. Didn't she, Nicky?' She looked at Nic, begging for pity with her eyes.

Nic looked ashamed and stood up from the second row. She nodded. 'It's true. She was very mean to Masha, sorry, I mean Nadiya. She threw her down the stairs because an agent saw her as Dorothy and wanted to offer her a part in a West End show. Just in the chorus, mind. Belinda left her there screaming at the bottom of the stairs. She was a cruel girl.'

I turned on Nic. 'And you did nothing to stop this? And you still idolised her? Well, shame on you for being a pathetic bystander.' I turned back to Nadiya. 'And poisoning me? I assume that was all part of keeping up the charade of someone trying to kill you after Belinda was dead.'

Nadiya looked at me. 'Wouldn't have been much of a loss if you *had* died.'

This garnered a few cries of outrage from the group. I stepped back a little; the coldness in her voice scared me.

She went on, looking at me with disdain as she spoke, 'Honestly, I just don't see what all the fuss is about you. All the men want to sleep with you and all the women want to be your friend.'

'What do you mean, fuss?'

She shook her head like a haughty show pony. 'I mean, I spent two fucking years dieting on cabbage and beetroot, did daily exercises to lengthen my spine, lifted weights, ran, treated my hair with chemicals so that people in this country, in the world of the television, would treat me with respect and admiration and not call me "fat Russian troll". And here you are, you're not very thin or pretty, you've no particular talent. What is it?'

Kelsey answered for me, 'It's because she's nice. People like people who are nice. That's all.'

I smiled at Kelsey, then turned back to Nadiya. 'If you hated me that much, why did you even demand that I investigate this? Why not just make Chris ask the police to help?'

Nadiya shrugged and smiled ruefully. 'I didn't think you would be any good. I actually thought you'd give up after I nearly killed you. I don't know why you didn't – you nearly died. I wanted people to believe I was really scared and rather than get in the police, who might have solved it, I thought I'd ask you. I thought you'd go chasing off on the wrong direction, think that Belinda's death was your fault and I would simply be OK. All I've wanted since I was fourteen and lying in agony at the bottom of that staircase was to kill her.

And now I have. And you might be cleverer than me and have caught me but I will always know that I had my revenge.'

Wow, that was a truly harsh reply. Employed for my apparent shitness. It was impressive how long she had planned this revenge and the effort she had taken to go undetected by both Belinda and Nic.

I could see Jacob and Audrey having a hurried and quiet conversation. They sprang to their feet and, stony-faced and professional, walked over to Nadiya and led her away. She went without protest with a stoic expression on her face. The rest of the group had a moment of stunned silence before erupting into a big gossiping hubbub. Chris jumped up and shouted unnecessarily, 'That's it, everyone, I hope you've found some closure.'

He shook my hand and clasped me warmly on the arm. 'Cherry, that was amazing. I've no idea how you worked that one out and got her to confess. This is gunna be one amazing show. Let's pencil in a meeting after Christmas, yeah?'

'Sure,' I replied, 'you know where I am. See you later.'

I almost ran out of the doors to the studio, down the corridor and into the car park. It was cool and dark and felt nice on my face. I found it hard to believe that someone could burn with hatred for that long. Life was too short to go around bearing other people ill will. I looked back at the building – it had nearly killed me but my work here was done.

'Cherry, wait.'

Jacob, what a surprise. I turned round. 'What?'

'You were brilliant in there. So cool even when Nadiya was well rude. I just wanted to say I've never thought you were shit. You've always been brilliant. You're kind and brave and funny and if anyone murdered me, I'd trust you to find out who did it.'

'Right, well, best put that one in your will for Kim to find, then.'

He shook his head. 'Don't. Look, I don't want to be with Kim, I'm in love with you. I can't stop being in love with you. I forgive you for sleeping with Felix. Please, let's give us another go?'

I walked up to him so we were nose to slightly swollen nose and then I kissed him. The world spun, my tummy dropped into my feet and shot back up again like a fairground ride and I couldn't get close enough to him. I wanted to kiss him so much that we actually just became one living kissing thing. I don't know how long we stood like that, but I knew it had to end. I pulled away and said, 'That was a kiss goodbye, Jacob.'

'What?'

'I can't go on being on and off and back on again. My heart can't cope with it.'

'Cherry, what do you mean? What about me? I said I forgive you.'

'I mean, I don't want to be with you. We tried it and it didn't work out. And that's that.' I turned and walked away. 'And one more thing: I didn't do anything that *needed* forgiving. In fact, I forgive you for being you!'

'What?'

But he was too late.

I got into my car and drove away, leaving him standing in the car park trying to figure out what just happened. I wasn't even entirely sure myself.

Like my nose, my heart would heal over and I would start again. For now, I had a big fat cheque in my pocket from Chris that needed paying in and a peaceful holiday to book for January, when no one wanted cake.

Acknowledgements

I would like to thank everyone who helped me with the writing of this book. Particular thanks must go to Abbie Headon for her outstanding editing and continued enthusiasm for Cherry and also Hattie Grunwald; my equally enthusiastic agent at The Blair Partnership.

I would also like to thank Pete Duckworth and Fanny Emily Lewis at Duckworth Books and Becca Allen for her incredibly close eye for detail.

Since I know nothing about dancing or music, I had to enlist some expert help so a big thank you to Richard Harvey for explaining beats in bars and various tempos to me and also to Jane Corby for her knowledge of how ankle injuries would affect one's dancing. Thanks to Andres Gutierrez and Denis Dildayev for some quick Russian advice. Any mistakes here are totally mine.

Thank you to the real-life people whose names I have stolen- especially Liz Farley and Nic Johnston. And to the people who've loaned me their names for a second time round even after they'd read the first one; Thomas Hodson, Mark Byrne and Matthew Shepherd.

Thank you to Melissa for giving me the time and space to write – despite the very challenging circumstances!

Also Available

Cherry Slice

Reality TV turns deadly in Cherry Hinton's first case

When Kenny Thorpe, a contestant on Expose TV's *Big Blubber*, the hot new celebrity weight-loss show, is murdered on live television in front of three million viewers, the case seems pretty watertight. After all, everyone saw Martin do it – didn't they?

Cherry Hinton knows there's more to this than meets the eye. As an investigative reporter, she went undercover on dating show *Caravan of Love*... but after getting in too deep with one of the other contestants, she was caught knickerless in front of the nation. Humiliated, fired and heartbroken, she has fled to Brentwood, where she opens a cake shop, and tries to forget all about Expose.

Until Kenny Thorpe's sister walks into her shop with a letter that turns Cherry's world upside down. Is Martin innocent? How is infamous gangster Leon Solent involved? Is Expose to blame, and is there a killer still on the loose?

Cherry is the only one in a position to find out.

A Cherry PI Mystery, Volume 1

OUT NOW

About the Author

Jennifer Stone was born in Essex and spent her formative years living within its borders and enjoying the delights of the multiple night clubs and alcopop-swigging opportunities available. After a stint in North Wales acquiring a degree and a further spell in Leeds, training to be a teacher, she returned to the south of England to teach English in a variety of schools. She is currently head of English at a boarding school in Suffolk and has just completed her MA in Creative Writing (Crime) at UEA. She lives with her wife and their small son.

Note from the Publisher

To receive updates on new releases in the Cherry PI Mystery Series – plus special offers and news of other humorous fiction series to make you smile – sign up now to the Farrago mailing list at farragobooks.com/sign-up.